by the same author

fiction
GRAVITY: STORIES

non-fiction
ARIEL'S GIFT: TED HUGHES, SYLVIA PLATH AND
THE STORY OF BIRTHDAY LETTERS

SEIZURE

Erica Wagner

faber and faber

First published in 2007
by Faber and Faber Limited
3 Queen Square London WC1N 3AU

Typeset by Faber and Faber Limited
Printed in England by Mackays of Chatham, plc

A CIP record for this book
is available from the British Library

ISBN 978–0–571–22759–4

2 4 6 8 10 9 7 5 3 1

There is a lipstick on the dresser, by the cracked and clouded mirror. A tube of mock-tortoiseshell, twined with a relief of blossoms, a dull gold band where the lid can be drawn off with a sucking pop. In faded letters, just legible, on its base: Miss Firecracker. Two twists and then a finger of scarlet wax: red as blame. My breath blurs the air. It is cold here. The fire makes only a little warmth.

Whose face in the glass? It could be hers. I have tucked the photograph into the wooden frame: a black and white portrait, formal, a string of pearls, eyelashes retouched with a long fine brush. A closed-mouth smile, like mine. A dark clean gaze: you would call it candid, perhaps, unless you knew it was not. Our bones. Our eyes. Our throats.

I take the lipstick and press it to my mouth. Age has congealed it, made it sticky and chalky all at once, but I stretch my face and press, staining my lips with the colour. How easily we read wavelengths into monochrome: I know my lips match hers. I don't remember that mouth kissing me. I don't remember the smell of her perfume; I don't remember the click of those pearls near my ear as she kissed me goodnight. I have none of it. A sweet, chemical taste on the edge of my tongue.

I have something else, now.

My eyes half-shut, I tilt my head. Twins. The sky is

I

leached of colour so that out of the little window there is only black and white, the trees shadows against the shrouded sky. This could be a cut-out landscape, a set. The sea, with its secrets and seals, beyond. Here is my red mouth, here is blood unwashed from the blade of his knife, and his perfect stillness, his closed eyes.

CHAPTER ONE

Stephen whispered into her ear as quiet swept across the gathering in the vaulted chambers below the street: 'Vintage, that dress?' A question, but the kind of thing he would know. The place lit with tall iron candelabra and tea-lights serried against the edges of the brick. The slight smell of damp was not unpleasant; it was cool and pure. There weren't many of them, sixty or so guests gathered on a sweep of black seats; she held her hands in her lap, nodded in answer to his question, her hair brushing against the line of his jaw.

The bride took her place in the centre of the aisle, her long back with a fishtail of ivory silk flowing down it, an exclamation in the muted light. Here I begin, here is what is new, here is the truth. Janet shifted; her shoulder pressed against Stephen's and then she leant away, took a deep breath of the moist air.

He turned his head, looked at her, raised his eyebrow. She smiled.

No *dearly beloved*. The groom, his thick beard oddly lupine on his youthful face, reading Whitman. One of the candles on the floor guttered out, and pale smoke floated up past the brick. *The greatest of these is love.*

She felt it all begin to recede. A breath of cold metal, high in the back of her throat. The wrong end of a telescope.

Was he watching her? She dug her nails into her wrist to hold herself in place, felt her chest rise and fall. She would not go over the edge of it. She would resist.

He was not watching. Janet saw his lifted face, his carved profile, his comfort that had made her so comfortable, the ease that had brought her ease. She could see it all, but from a distance, the distance of herself as she made her own electricity, this lightshow that she couldn't control. It flickered and ticked, thrummed in her, danced itself. She remembered the long metal tube she'd lain in, the hammer of magnets, frozen in the noise and then the picture of her brain, laid out in grey and black slices against the blinding fluorescence of a hospital lamp.

She must have moved, or drawn breath: he heard and shifted. What did he see? Even in this opening of time she could imagine her face changed into some other, an animal's, a creature's, something not human. Her eyes wide, the long slits of pupils, her teeth against the air. No. He put his hand over hers where she cut at her own skin; *hard*, she whispered, and felt his pressure increase, holding her still, holding her down, holding her into herself. *The greatest of these is love.*

There was applause. Something had happened. The metal breath drew back, a steel sea receding, and Janet relaxed, her body let out of itself, suddenly tired, suddenly warm. His arm around her shoulder, his mouth on her temple. Again? And she nodded.

Her hands flat and limp. He pushed a lock of her hair behind her ears, as if she were a child. There was enough noise now, a scraping back of chairs, they could speak. 'Do you want to go?' he asked. 'Was it bad?'

'It's always bad,' she said. 'And not bad. I know what it is. There's nothing to it. It's just – bad, that's all. Not good.'

She sighed. 'I didn't think they'd start again. I thought they were over.'

'Come on,' he said. 'I'll take you home. No one will mind.'

'Of course they will,' she said. 'I used to look after Adam. They'd mind. We'll stay to dinner.'

'All right,' he said. He brought her a glass of water, which she drank. She wondered at the comfort of water, given in extremity to the bereaved, offered in the face of distress. *Here: it's what we're all made of. We're just the same.* Was that it?

At dinner they were seated at opposite ends of a table. Soup to begin, fish, red meat, good wine. The seizure had left Janet with a thin ache behind her eyes and she knew she should not drink, but she did. Not too much. Two seats down from her, the groom's mother, Janet's friend Shelley, all in black with a stack of white pearls at her neck, glowing with – achievement, perhaps. Janet looked around, the paintings on the walls, the moulded ceilings, the red and cream roses strewn on the mantelpiece of this grand room that had once served some authentic purpose but was now a venue, an echo chamber of celebration. The marriage of Adam, yes, but also the achievement of this evening, something crystalline and perfected. No mess: what was before, what would come after had no place here.

Stephen's dark head was bent towards the woman on his left. She liked to watch him, always, the grace of him: the music he made was in his body and never left him. She could not hear what they were saying, but she could see the calibration of his smile, just enough, not quite the real thing; enough for the woman, a stranger with a chiffon scarf. He was good at this, charming those who required it, for whatever reason, in whatever circumstance. A memory of the first smile he had given her; then, she had not seen what it was. When it had changed into what she told herself was true – she couldn't have said, not quite. For a second her own distance pulled her from him, from his affection, his regard, his love. Then he caught her eye, and there he was, the one she knew. She was sure of that. His gaze cooled and relaxed her.

Silver on glass: speeches. Janet sat back. There was champagne in front of her now, rasping in her throat when she drank. She shifted her chair to listen: to the best man, sweet and loving the way men, she thought, are rarely loving to each other any more; the groom, loving too of those who had come here, those who could not, grateful and charming in his concern. The maid-of-honour, with her story of a long late drive, a small car, a chance meeting. The silence of the guests opened to let in their words and the words rose and filled the room.

Only the bride was silent. Janet watched her. She was a very pretty girl. Not beautiful, but very pretty, her neat face and small chin, her hair swept up plainly. Although she wore a wedding dress she looked unadorned. Janet had met her once before; they had spoken briefly. Janet had liked her, well enough. Now, with the ache behind her eyes, watching her silence, the bride's silence, she grew hot. Heat blossomed at the base of her throat and pricked her eyes: the heat of rage, at this silence, at this column of white, of dreamt purity, of the thing given away and taken again. The will abandoned, and gladly. Tears ran out of Janet's eyes and Shelley leant across, patted her hand, mouthed: *How many years ago?* and winked. Janet stretched her mouth to smile back. She was being ridiculous. Don't be ridiculous. It's a wedding. Everyone loves a wedding.

'Now let's go,' Janet said to Stephen as the guests rose and milled. He had come to find her, put his hand on the small of her back. 'I could use some air.'

The night was warm. Summer was not quite over, and a breeze came off the river. They walked east, in silence, through crowds and then into streetlamp half-dark, crossing puddles of light and shadow. They walked all the way home. By the cathedral, her shoes began to hurt, and so she took them off and felt the pavement rough under her feet.

'Be careful,' he said. He was a careful man.

'I will,' she said, and put one foot in front of the other, steadily.

It was nearly midnight by the time he turned the key in the lock. Egg-yolk light in the hallway, empty coats waiting on hooks, yesterday's newspaper on the kitchen table. Nothing remarkable, nothing strange. The storm in her head had left her with its particular exhaustion; the headache had gone, but she was drained, and as she shed her clothes – draping them as she went, carelessly, her shawl over a newel post, the dress over a chair, her shoes left by the door – she imagined that without them she might be invisible, or at least translucent. She pulled herself up the stairs, trailing her hand along the smooth dark wood of the banister shining with wax, with years of palms. Strangers holding her hand through the wood, through time.

Stephen was pulling off his tie, standing by the blinking eye of the answerphone. He took off his jacket, set it neatly on a hanger.

'Go ahead,' she said to him, jutting her chin at the message machine, and he pushed the button.

'Hey Janet, hey Steve,' Jill's voice. 'Just wondering if you'd had a chance . . .'

7

'This is old,' Janet said. 'It's about that lunch she wanted to arrange. It's all set. I've written it down.'

'Good,' he said. 'Thanks.' They functioned smoothly as a unit; they hardly had to think about it. Back and forth, forth and back. It all just happened. It was good. Fast forward, he pressed.

'This is a message for Janet Ward,' said a voice she did not recognise. She looked at him: *Someone you know?* A shrug. 'My name is Ernest Jackson. I'm with Jackson, Thomas and Strang, solicitors. Would you do me the favour of telephoning me?' Smoothly Stephen reached for a pen and a piece of paper, wrote down the digits in his graceful, slanting hand. A hiss of tape, for a pause. 'Thank you very much, Miss Ward. I'll look forward to your call.'

The machine switched off. They stood and looked at it, as if it were keeping something from them.

'What's that about, do you suppose?' she asked.

'Message for you,' he said. 'I don't know.'

'Something from work, is all I can think,' she said. 'To do with – I don't know, the planning permission or something.'

'For the Centre? I thought that was sorted.'

'So did I,' she said. 'But you never know. Christ,' she said. 'I'm shattered. That poor woman.'

'Who?' He'd gone into the bathroom, his voice against the tile.

'Alex.'

'The bride? Why? I thought you liked him . . . liked them all.' The sound of water running. Janet slipped a T-shirt over her head, too tired to shower.

'Oh, I do. It's just the silence that gets to me. She sat there. Got given away. Everyone talking but her.'

'They don't have to say *obey* any more, you know.' She could hear the smile in his voice; only now she found herself wondering which of his smiles it might be. His words were so easy and clean. 'Anyone would think you were some kind of feminist.'

In bed now, she pulled the duvet over herself, settled her reading glasses on the end of her nose, looked at the stack of funding reports on the bedside table and sighed. He liked this conversation, one they'd had before in different forms; themes and variations, as in his music. She was tired, and suddenly wanted nothing at all. Stephen came out of the bathroom and saw her leafing through the reports.

'For heaven's sake,' he said. He put his hand over hers, took it off the papers, kissed it.

'I guess I am some kind of feminist,' she said.

'One that works too hard. You know those things mean that at least you should take it easy.' Things. Not seizures. A deflection, a diminution. 'You know – a wedding like that –'

'What?'

'Well. It might make a certain kind of fellow romantic. But "that poor woman" is somewhat off-putting.'

Outside, a siren; a too-loud television across the street. Late night talk, footsteps, laughter: a voice saying, you're joking. 'You're not going to ask me to marry you, are you?' She pulled her glasses down lower on her nose and stared hard at him, smiling.

'I guess not,' he said.

* * *

I dreamt I went to my mother's grave. I knew where it was; there was no journey, I was simply there, in a cemetery, a place not distinguished, orderly, with clean stones and young trees. Nothing gothic or spooky: the sort of cemetery

9

you pass as you're heading out of town on a train, iron railings that go on and on, neat rows of stones, all much the same size and shape, regimented loss, regulated grief. Or a reminder of the absence of either: for as I walk between them, along the grass to where I know she is, I feel nearly nothing, or only what one might feel on an errand of obligation, the emotion of a tea-time visit to an elderly aunt. My mother. Her grave. There it is.

She is sitting up. I can't see what is written on her gravestone because she is resting against it, as if it were the headboard of a bed. A carpet of grass is laid over her lap like a rug, and her hands are folded on top of it. In the twilight – for it is twilight, I remember that now, and there is a narrow slice of moon hanging above the anodyne plane trees – I can see manicured threads of damp, green grass tufting through her fingers. A gold wedding ring, loose below her knuckle. How old is she? Do I peer at her, to see? That I can't remember. Young then, or not aged: a woman, a woman. Black hair, falling loose around her shoulders over a plain white nightgown, trimmed with delicate lace. I have never seen her in such a thing, of course, never even seen a picture of her in such a thing: have never owned one myself. Yet there it is, its square, worked neck, its ruched sleeves. There is no rise and fall of her chest, no breath as I approach her: but when I come closer, in the air-tread of sleep, she blinks her dark eyes at me and smiles. Pale, her skin. But I am not afraid. She is not a corpse; that is not how it seems to me. I stand over her. Her head tips up to look at me. Then her mouth opens and she speaks, although her lips do not move. Then I am afraid, standing on the border between dream and nightmare.

'You found me,' she says.

'I wasn't looking,' I say.

'But here I am.' She lifts her hands from her lap, holds them out, gesturing at the headstones, the trees. 'All this.'

'All what?' Do I recall this right? Do we know, in our dreams, what we do not know, or ought to know?

'Everything.' The tilt of her neck is like a marionette's. It is so quiet, and I wonder if she can see something I cannot: surely she can, for she is dead and I am not. Her eyes gleam in the wan and fading light. I squat on my haunches to be closer to her, but I do not reach out to touch her. The thin print of lines on her brow, just visible; her fingernails, like opals. She is beautiful. Her beauty makes my fear fall away, and I lean into her, turn my head to see where her gaze is directed. White gravel between the trees, shining. 'Look,' she says.

A rush, then. An opening, as if all the blood in my body has run into my heart at once. A wind rises up lightly and blows against my face: someone is walking along the gravel path and I can hear the even tread, though I can't see anything, whether because of the gloom or because there is nothing there to see, I don't know. But I can feel the steps like the beat in my chest, and what I know then is hope, a blind surge of it, a flight rising up and making me reach out to take my mother's hand as she sits so composed, so still in her grave, where I can be near her at last. We are about to touch, and then I wake.

* * *

Ernest Jackson: Jackson, Thomas and Strang. Janet had scribbled the number down on a slip of paper, stuffed it into her wallet; the next morning, pulling out a note to buy her morning shot of coffee, there it was. It was midday before she rang him, though, the day scrambling out of her grasp.

'Jackson, Thomas and Strang,' the syllables almost without meaning in the telephonist's chant.

'Ernest Jackson, please.'

'Who may I say is calling?'

'Janet Ward.'

'Hold the line, please.'

She held, moving the phone just away from her ear so the tinny Vivaldi was less insistent. Below, someone was walking across the square below the Centre, eating a sandwich; two paper napkins fluttered off behind like doves.

'Miss Ward. Thank you for calling. Ernest Jackson.'

'Ah – thank you,' said Janet, realising she had given very little thought to what she might say. 'May I – may I ask what this is about?'

'Of course you may. That's the point of this, if you'll forgive me.' What would Ernest Jackson look like? A light voice, slightly nasal, assuredly professional. A trace of an accent that did not belong to this city, an accent not completely eliminated but suppressed all the same. French cuffs or button sleeves? She had nothing to go on. She knew nothing at all.

'You are the daughter of Mr Benjamin Nicholls Ward and Mrs Margaret Justice Ward?'

The room grew very still. To be sure, there were the sounds of the street, the sounds of the corridor, Ellen and Nick at the coffee machine, she could hear them, Ellen laughing suddenly, the gurgle of the ancient plumbing, a train on its track. The quotidian. But a hollow within it at the sound of her parents' names.

'I . . .' She almost put the phone down. Later, would she remember that? It all could have stopped. She could never have known. Two sides of a coin. Choose one path, choose another. Travel this way or turn back. A figure waiting at a crossroads.

'Miss Ward?'

'Yes, I'm here. Yes. Yes, I am.'

'Consequent to your mother's death, you've inherited a small property. That's what this phone call is about. We'll need to arrange a formal transfer of the property to you. When would it be convenient to meet?'

'Consequent to my . . .' For one irrational moment she wondered if he was speaking another language. Or if there was another Janet Ward, daughter of Benjamin Nicholls Ward and Margaret Justice Ward. They were not such uncommon names. 'My mother . . .' And then she laughed.

'You were saying?' Ernest Jackson was not laughing.

'Mr Jackson, my mother died years ago. Why is this just coming to light now?'

'Your mother died three weeks ago, Miss Ward.' His voice so flat, so matter-of-fact. 'I'm sorry if you were under a different apprehension.'

Her own hand was cool on her hot forehead. She did not speak for a little while. This time, he did not try to coax her into words. Had he done this before? Perhaps this kind of thing happened all the time. Perhaps he made several of these calls every week.

'I was,' she said. 'I was under a different apprehension.' Apprehension. Apprehensive. 'May we meet this evening?'

In the early dusk she walked to his office, heading west instead of east, as she had walked with Stephen the night before, through the blue-orange pall that fell over the city as the evening drew in. It might rain; the dingy trees, cramped in their concrete pens, showed the undersides of their leaves as if they were still wild things.

Jackson, Thomas and Strang was in that part of the city where such offices are, where the grey stone buildings were old and not too tall, and where narrow alleyways scuttled away from the broad streets. Through one such alleyway she found a courtyard, a door, a brass bell and wide wooden stairs worn down in the middle of their treads. By the time she arrived it had just gone seven; everyone had left except Ernest Jackson, who stood at the top of the stairs and waited for her.

French cuffs, then. Not that she cared any more, but she noticed, the cuffs and the neat beard around his mouth. 'Come in, come in,' he said, extending an arm past her shoulder but not touching her, a phantom embrace. 'May I get you a glass of water?'

Water again. 'You don't have anything stronger?' She tried to smile, caught between the self she was at work and the self she would have to be here – but which self was that, exactly? The motherless girl no longer motherless – or at least until three weeks ago. Who was she?

Jackson raised an eyebrow. 'Tea,' he said.

'Tea would be lovely.'

He showed her into his office and went to boil the kettle himself. Janet lowered herself into the chair across from his desk, a big old leather chair with wings that looked much more comfortable than it actually was. A window looked out over the darkening yard; she could see the face of a clock. Five minutes past seven; six. No second hand, no jerk of the minute hand. She did not see the clock move but still it did. Things changed. You didn't see them changing, but they changed.

He knocked before he entered, knocked on his own office door. But he didn't pause, just knocked and in he came with a single cup of tea, a proper cup with a saucer, and nothing for himself. He set it down on the far edge of his desk, where she could reach it from the chair, and settled himself down across from her.

'I hope I didn't keep you too late,' Janet said.

'Oh no,' he said. 'Don't worry about that.' He glanced down at the pile of papers on his desk. He reminded Janet of a dog – a good kind of dog, clever, like a red setter, perhaps, but a dog all the same. It was not a bad quality in a solicitor, she thought. Dogged. There must be a good reason for the word. He had an open face. She would like to think she could trust him. But she did not know if that was true.

He took a folder from the top of the pile, a brown folder tied with a brown ribbon. He pulled at the loose knot; it gave itself up, and from the opened folder he took a stiff bound sheaf of papers which he handed across to her. Janet looked down at it, but didn't see it.

'What is this?'

'Your mother's will.' He spoke slowly now, as if he were talking to a child. She felt like a child. She would allow him to speak to her in this way, she would not object. *I am a grown woman with responsibilities, with a job, with a life, my own life which I have made*: but suddenly that life seemed provisional, rescinded. She looked not at the paper, but at his calm brown eyes. 'Frankly, there wasn't much to leave,' he said. 'But this property is – well, not insignificant, at any rate. And it was left in trust for you.'

Janet leafed through the will; all she saw were legal terms, stiff as coffin timber, that meant little to her. Heretofore. The above-mentioned. The aforesaid. Black and white lines like marching ants.

'What property? What does all this mean? How did she – how did you – find me?'

He breathed in, as if sorting and ordering her swift questions before he ventured his answer. One thing at a time, she could almost hear him think.

'It was simple to discover your whereabouts,' he said. He dusted some invisible speck off his sleeve, brushing off the accomplishment of finding her. 'In fact, all but your most recent address was included in the documentation.'

'She – she knew where I was?' Janet could not hide her astonishment.

'Apparently,' said Ernest Jackson. *Your estrangement from your mother is not my business.* 'And it means – well, it means, if I may say, that you have an unexpected little windfall.' *See? Good news. Always look on the bright side.* There was a box of tissues on his desk. Her cup of tea was getting cold. She took a swallow, downing the hard crust of her anger, her surprise.

Now the clock outside the window said twenty minutes past seven. Stephen might be home; she had left a message that she would go to see the lawyer after work. She had not told him about what. Planning permission was what she had left him with. He would be calm, as he always was; he would begin to make the supper. What was there for supper? Cold wine in the fridge, the beading of moisture on the bottle as it sat on the kitchen counter. Stephen pouring a glass for himself, turning on the radio.

'If you turn to the last page,' said Mr Jackson, peering over his desk at her hands holding the document, 'you'll see. It's about –' he looked at some notes he had on his desk, 'three hundred miles from here. North. By the sea. It has a name, I think. The Shieling.'

CHAPTER TWO

At five o'clock Tom pulled himself out from underneath the car. He didn't wear a watch, and from where he was he couldn't see any natural light, only the white fluorescence from the strip on the garage ceiling, the light from his lantern underneath the chassis. The hiss of the kettle told him the time: five o'clock and Pete always made the tea. The cupboards in the tiny kitchen – it was hardly that – opening and shutting; the cellophane racket of a packet of biscuits, the squeak the fridge door always made. He reached back, switched off the lantern, stood up and stretched his back.

'There you go,' Pete said. Handed him a thick white china mug that already had a stripe of grease on it. A rag to clean his hands: he picked it up from the cement floor and only smeared the oil into his fingers. The inside of the mug was clean; the tea tasted fine. Pete held out the packet of biscuits.

'Penny for 'em,' Pete said.

No answer. No answer to give. Only this sense. Like a wind from a different direction. Nothing to say. He shook his head. Get out of it. 'Might go for a drink tonight,' he said. 'At The Fisherman. Fancy?'

'Could be,' Pete said. 'Got to ask the wife, I reckon.'

'Right you are,' he said.

Pete slurped from his mug, set it down on a tottering stack of old Yellow Pages. The place was a mess, mostly, strewn with bits of metal, gleaming and rusting jumbled together, cans of grease, cans of paint, brushes whose bristles had hardened until they were stiff as their wooden handles; jacks, spare tyres, a couple of rotten mufflers. Pete's beard scraggled down his neck; he was a hoarder, a pack rat. It was useful. Things could go unnoticed. He didn't care, as long as the work got done. 'Better pay you, then,' Pete said.

From a drawer he pulled a stack of old notes, counted the cash, handed it over, put the cash straight back in the drawer.

'You could get robbed sometime, you know. Anyone could get at that.'

Pete laughed. 'Place is locked.'

'Locks don't keep anyone out.'

''Spect not. You would, though,' Pete said. 'Scare the crap out of any robber, you would.'

He felt the blood rise in his neck.

'I don't care,' Pete said. 'If you were going to rob from me you'd a done it by now, I guess. Don't you?'

'I could be biding my time,' he said. Ventured a smile. Held the mug tight in his hands.

'Oh yeah,' Pete said. 'I guess you could be. Well.' He grinned. Reached back in the drawer, took out the cash, wadded it, stuffed it in his pocket. 'Feel better? Guess the drinks are on me tonight, then.'

'Guess so.'

Pete clapped him on the shoulder, hot moist hands, the thud of flesh. A hollow in the pit of his stomach. He was hungry. Better get something to eat before he started drinking.

Pete handed over the key to the place. 'Lock up, will you? See you – I don't know. Nine?'

'All right,' he said.

'Watch yourself, Tom,' Pete said. 'See you later.'

And so Tom locked up, the windows, the doors. Turning off the lights so there was nothing but a thin swim of twilight drifting through the dirty window glass – the openings high and small – to make the metal shine, what metal there was that wasn't eaten and scarred. He heard the slamming of Pete's car door, the engine turning over, the scrape of gravel, the machine-sound fading to a whine over the little hills, inland, where Pete's house was lit and warm. Winter was coming. Already he could feel the threat of it coming off the sea, the cold breath, the knife-edged damp.

Round the other side of the garage was a shed; he walked there now. On its swollen door was a combination padlock, brand new. He clicked the numbers with his greasy thumb and the bolt sprang; he left it hanging off the latch and went in. In the darkness, he moved easily, finding the oil lamp that sat on a shelf by the window, through the pane of which came, now, deep violet light. A lighter in his pocket. The glass chimney of the lantern lifted off, the wick lit, the orange flame with its heart black-and-blue. He closed the door behind him and pulled it shut. There was a latch on the other side of the door, a padlock too. This he clicked home. He knew no one would come. Still, he would not take the risk.

* * *

Once upon a time, a time as long ago as never and near enough to now, a woman stood at a threshold and looked out at the sea. The wood of her own door was smooth

19

beneath her palm, the stone of her own floor was firm beneath her feet. But on the horizon she could see a ship, the white sails of a ship against the sky – like flecks of snow against the sky, though it was high summer and her garden was thick with roses, the red and the white twined together.

Who was in the ship? the boy, Tom, says.

I'm coming to that, she answers. *Shhh.*

She stood at her threshold, watching the sea, watching the ship. And soon the ship came into harbour, drew up to the dock: a fine ship she was, the decks scrubbed with holy-stone, the rigging tight, canvas mended with the neat fast stitches of sailors. The woman cooked a supper, she scrubbed a shirt, she rocked the baby that lay in the cradle cooing and crying, but all the while her mind was on the sea and on the ship.

Was it a boy or a girl, the baby? asks the boy.

A girl, she answers. *A little baby girl.* And she kisses the top of the boy's head.

She had her back to the door when the knock came, but she felt it in her spine, in all the bones of her legs going down to the wooden soles of her shoes. It knocked against her ribs and shoulders: against her breath, against her heart. The baby was sleeping. She opened the door.

My husband's at sea, the woman said to the man who threw his shadow into her house. The morning was behind him, edging him with light but setting his face in darkness. She didn't need to see his face: she knew it like her own.

So he's at sea, came the answer. And now I'm not.

Seven years is a long time, she said.

Were you counting the days?

Only the hours, she replied. Their talk came easy and free.

He didn't step over the door. He looked her up and down, this seven-years-gone man, and saw her clothes a little patched and darned, her hands a little rough, her hair pulled back tight from her forehead, good wife that she was. She looked him up and down and saw the dark wing of his hair, the velvet at his collar, the gleaming skin of his leather boots with their fine thin soles. And then this man smiled, and this woman smiled, and in that one instant each reached for the other's hand.

You'll come? he said.

Of course. And she wiped her hands on her apron, stepped back into the room, banked the fire, folded the cloth on the table. The baby still slept, swaddled tight, rocking, and she knelt down beside the cradle and laid her hand on its wooden edge but did not touch the child. She watched the baby breathe. Then she stood. She walked out, over the threshold, she shut the door behind her and the morning sun shone on its closed face. The man saw the set of her jaw and as they walked away from the house he did not speak a while. Finally he said: It's all for you. All I have. All I've got.

I know, she answered. And on they walked, down the winding path to the harbour, to the sea, to the ship.

She left the baby? The boy stares up at her in the quiet she has made.

She did, the woman says.

You won't leave me?

Never. She kisses him again. *I'll never leave you.* But the story's not over, she says.

* * *

There were lights, too, in the shed; it wasn't just the oil lamp. He knew perfectly well that was a conceit: he liked the glow of its flame and its slick hot scent. Sometimes he switched on the light; but not tonight – the last light from the sky had not yet gone, and he liked, too, to work just by the blue-white flame of the torch. On the wall hung his mask, the thick glass over his eyes, hooking over the back of his head; heavy gloves, a leather apron scarred with burns, black spots and streaks. When the sparks fell on the apron the smell was of burning skin, staining the clean white flare of the acetylene.

On the metal bench he'd made were shards and scraps of iron and steel, not so different from some that lay in the garage; but these had mostly been salvaged from dumps and bins – and sometimes too from the sea. He liked the sea-saved metal, bleakly pitted by salt and rolled by the waves: he always imagined more stories in the scrap he lifted off the shore. You had to pick the stuff up carefully – more than once he'd gashed himself on some hidden jag, the red iron of his blood flowing over the rust-red of his find – and then you could turn it over and guess what had made that tear, that series of holes, that dent as if a spike had been driven hard into the side of something. The side of what? You could never tell. Piracy, a wreck, something sheared off suddenly in the night, in a heavy gale, a driving rain, the men with their oilskins (a weird, daisy-bright in the light from flares and emergency generators) fighting the heel of the ship, the drag of the sea. Splitting, sinking. Nothing would change the nature of the sea. It would fight back, harder. So he liked the sea iron.

The bent steel door of a pickup. Stray piping from someone's new kitchen. He was not indiscriminate. Some metal spoke and some didn't, some louder than other sorts. He would listen to it all. He gathered and trawled until the shed looked like a kind of hangar where some machine of unknown use and origin had been dismantled. Perhaps that was true. Now in the half-light he moved among his finds, choosing and discarding, kicking with the toe of his boot, finally bending to pick up this one or that one. A piece of fender, still streaked with paint the colour of woad; a fine coil of copper, greening at its edges. The torch fired up, the hard pop of the acetylene gas; hot orange bluing as the oxygen flowed into it. A feather of turquoise heat and a ball of whiteness as the metal cut, heating up through violet, to red, to white and then falling away from itself. With his gloved hand he reached for one of the brazing rods he kept by the bench; when he joined metal to metal he liked to watch the thick seam form like a scar. The flame, nearly silent, streamed from the torch, from his hands as he turned the material this way and that, finding where the seam asked to be.

He went into the work. He didn't wear a watch, but he would emerge in time to meet Pete for that drink at The Fisherman. He wanted a drink, though he didn't always. The last weeks hadn't been easy; he knew he stood at the edge of something, but he couldn't see over, couldn't see what was on the other side. Just as he thought it was getting better, it got worse, and now the buzz in his head was almost constant, making him clumsy and careless. Pete's voice calling out: Tom? Tom? Three times, or four, before he heard.

A year since he'd been here, now, a little more. It had been good. He hadn't wanted to keep away any more: he'd wanted to see the beginning of it all, that's how he thought of it. When he looked back it was the ordinariness of everything that had startled him. He had spent those first days looking, lurking, as if something might be revealed to him or about him – but nothing. He went about his business. They went about theirs. Stopping by the garage for a fill-up, Pete's wary greeting, the gradual acceptance. Someone had brought in a little MG, needed it fixed by the day before yesterday – this was last spring, when it was just getting warm and the southerners started to come to play on the links by the water or eat hot fried fish sitting on a sea wall. I can do that, Tom said. It's your oil pump. Look. And he showed the man, who stood leaning on a big golf umbrella, his face flushed from the wind or something else, Tom couldn't know and didn't care. I don't mind, he said to Pete. I'm cheap. Then he laughed, and so did the man with the MG, too loudly.

Pete scraping at his beard, a characteristic gesture, he knew by now. That was it. Pete paid him cash and didn't ask many questions. Money to eat, money to drink, enough to do and the ground under his feet, the sea always in the edge of his vision, the blue-grey of its great eye on him. He'd never liked living inland; it was like living behind a high wall to him. As he worked, the hiss of his torch echoed the hiss of the waves on the sand, rushing up, falling back, always allowing of another possibility, another opportunity. Come and go, ebb and flow.

He bent and turned the cock that stopped the flow of gas; the white flame sank back and died. Under his mask the sweat ran down the side of his face and his palms were damp in his leather gloves. In front of him his shard of steel, not too much altered yet; the gash in its centre gazing up at him blindly. He ran his thumb along its edge, felt the bite of it against his skin.

It was dark now, time to go. The oil lamp guttering, needing more fuel. He pulled a wool jacket off a hook on the wall and went to the lock on the door, turned its barrels, unclasped the shackle. Shoving his hand in the sleeve of his jacket he lifted the glass of the lamp and blew on the wick. The darkness was heavy around him. He didn't mind the dark; he liked it. Though more than once, tonight, as he walked along the edge of the metalled road towards The Fisherman, he turned to look behind him as if he might see someone following. There was no one, and no sound of footsteps other than his own. But the feeling of something coming would not go away.

* * *

Tell me about the ship, says the boy.

You like the ship, the woman says. *You always like the ship*.

I do, says the boy. *Tell me.*

Shipshape, the woman says. *Shipshape, that's what they say, isn't it?*

And so it was. You remember: the decks – holystoned bright, the rigging tight –*What's holystone?* asks the boy.

I don't know, she says. *I don't. But it's what you use to clean the deck of a ship. Shhh. Listen.*

Holystoned bright, the rigging tight, black paint, the canvas sails so well stitched they looked as fine as silk. And what was in the ship? All sorts. Fine things to eat –

Like what? The boy is always hungry, greedy.

Ham. Jam. Cream. Roast chickens. Fruit from the far corners of the earth, mangosteens, rambutans, durian, mandarins; dried fruit too, figs and apricots and sweet black cherries. Cheese, strong cheese, with thick veins of blue running through, and smoked fish, salmon the colour of the dawn and sable like fine-grained wood.

25

Candy?

Chocolate. Dried orange peel dipped in chocolate. Turkish delight. Liquorice whips. Sherbet lemons. *What else, do you think?*

Peppermint sticks.

Peppermint sticks, then, there were certainly peppermint sticks.

And when the woman climbed aboard the ship, that was the first thing she saw – peppermint sticks in a dish, set by the mainmast, and she took one for her pocket and one for her mouth. But it wasn't only good things to eat on the ship; there was gold, too, and jewels, in chests and boxes and barrels, and beautiful silks for the woman to wear and dainty leather shoes. She had never seen the like.

You've done well in seven years, she said to him.

Except that I was missing you, he said, and stood at the helm. It was a bright day with a good breeze that pushed against the canvas of the sails; the ship strained against the anchor, as if she were longing to go, to be set free, to ride on the wild green sea. And the woman was so pleased to be aboard – with all that candy, all that gold, all those dresses – that she didn't think to wonder how the ship might get under way: for there was no one on board but her and her handsome, dark-haired gentleman. There were no sailors to climb the rigging or run below; there was no cabin boy; no cat. Love is blind. You don't always see what's in front of your eyes.

Tom says nothing. The woman, the storyteller, is not looking at him, but at something far away. He is in his bed, with his feet warm under the sheets and woollen blankets. He is happy. He is not going to break the spell. He will not think about the baby left behind. He thinks of the candy and the gold. The spell is a good one, strong.

No cat, no cabin boy, no sailors. And the woman didn't see. That night, as she slept in a bed with white satin sheets and a cover of fine goosedown, the anchor chain rose up into the belly of the ship, the sails filled with a good wind, and with the moon riding high in a dark sky streaked with rags and scraps of cloud, the vessel with its two passengers and rich cargo slipped away from the harbour and set out for the open sea.

The boy blinks. She kisses him.

Finish the story, he says.

You could have another story, the woman says. *I don't feel like telling the rest tonight.*

You promised, he says. *I want to know what happens.*

You already know, she says.

The boy doesn't say anything. He knows and he doesn't know. That's how her stories work. He never knows. He loves her.

There is quiet. She puts her hand to the blanket around him, tucks it, tidies it, though it needs neither tucking nor tidying. *It's not a very good bedtime story, really,* she says.

Still he doesn't say anything, and the woman smiles.

For seven days and seven nights the boat sailed away on the open ocean. The woman slept and the woman woke, and when she woke her fine gentleman stood at the helm, steering the ship out towards the horizon. The sails, silver-white, were always perfectly set to catch the wind. Sometimes she would stand at the ship's bowsprit, right where the waves breasted against the prow, the water falling and unfurling ceaselessly, invisible patterns that near-hypnotized her with their surge and draw. She had a fur cloak now to draw round her: the darned, patched clothes she had left in had vanished. Although it was brisk the sun was warm and pleasant on the nape of her neck, and warm too was the knowledge of her fine gentleman's gaze upon her as he stood and steered the ship. The days were high-cast, blue, perfect: her heart had been let from its cage. The sea and the wind stirred her and changed her and the thoughts of her old life were blown out of her like morning mist.

But on the eighth day she emerged from below in her silk dress, her warm cloak, and drew the fur close about her: something had changed. Cloud smeared the edge of the horizon, grey and dirty like wool just cut from the sheep. She wore slippers of watered green silk; her toes were cold against the decking of the ship.

Not so fine today, she said to him. Still he stood at the wheel. He turned his head to look at her and the cold ran up from her feet to her heart, jarring on the rutted path of her spine. His face the same but not the same; his grin like something tossed in a corner of a graveyard, bone and tooth and hollow eye. She looked him up and she looked him down and she saw the crack in his fine leather boots, the calfskin buckled and split by what was within. Split, like her heart; cloven, as she had been from all that she had left behind. The baby cried, her little girl. Miles away, leagues away, across a wide, wild ocean, and yet the cry reached her over the wind so that she fell to the deck and screamed.

Hush, dear, he said, dropping near. His breath was hot in her ear. There's no one to hear. Look.

His hand gripped her arm above the elbow hard enough to bruise and he pulled her to her feet. The pain brought her back to herself and only then did she think: No sailors? No cabin boy? No cat? The blade of her wondering ran her through. Like a blade the ship cut through the dark sea, all sails set, though now the sky had gone from grey to brown and was darkening to black, rain flinging itself down and striking her nearly as hard as hail, soaking the white fur of her cloak, flattening her hair, running down into the hollow of her throat. The ship began to bow and plunge, and it might have been thunder or it might have been laughter she heard out of the ruined sky ripped by white electric glare.

He was a giant, says the boy.

That's right, the woman says. He is holding her hand now, their fingers twined like ivy.

She looked up. Her fine gentleman had become a giant, his head above the sails, his head above the topmast, his great feet – his hooves, splayed and clawlike – straddling the breadth of the poor little ship which still fought the tide but more sluggishly now, yawing with a drunken, damaged lurch, her belly filling with the sea.

The baby slept in her cradle. Her husband tended the fire. His tears fell on the embers and sizzled away, leaving nothing but salt.

She screamed again when he stamped his foot but her scream got sucked into the cold green sea that filled her belly too. A great crack and the keel of the ship split, a rending like the lightning that cut the air; then silence. She noticed the silence as the waves closed over her head and her silk dress clung heavy to her white skin and her eyes saw the last of the light as she travelled down and down, quite peaceful now in the stillness and the cold that was no longer cold but only what was familiar.

The baby slept in her cradle. Her husband tended the fire. She would be home soon. She would be home soon.

For a while the boy and the woman sit with their arms round each other. His hair, so unlike her own, is the colour of straw, almost of snow, and so fine; she curls a lock of it round her finger, over and over, twisting, twirling. His little mouth is against her neck; his every breath against the quick pulse in her throat.

It's a good story, he says at last. *She shouldn't have left that baby.*

No, says the woman. *No.*

* * *

Tom drank whisky; Pete drank beer. Tom couldn't be doing with all that liquid; every ten minutes Pete was out the back to piss. It was a Wednesday night and the place was quiet. The pair of lads from Home Farm down the road; Earldean polishing glasses behind the bar, a couple of golfers, they looked like, with their two big parrot-coloured umbrellas propped beside them. Just as Tom had approached the pub it had begun to spit a little with rain, cool flecks on his neck and forearms.

The lads played pool, then got bored, neither of them managing to pot the black as the two balls hared around the table at the end of their two games. They bought more drinks and Pete put his pint on the corner of the table. 'Come on,' he said. 'For the next round.'

One eye shut, imagining the trajectory of the creamy ball. He liked the game, though he wasn't that good at it; he liked the stark colours and the good weight of the balls, the crack of the break like something opening up. After two drinks (Pete won the first game) he felt more relaxed, and so he won the next, and the whisky warmed and loosened him. Stretching his arms, stretching his back, click and click and click.

'Like Paul fucking Newman,' said Pete, when he potted the black again, right in the centre pocket. 'Go on,' and he walked to the bar. 'One more.'

'No thanks,' Tom said. 'I should go.'

'If you're late tomorrow, you know,' Pete said, 'I won't tell the boss.' His head back, laughing. His wet, yellow teeth and thick tongue.

'It's all right,' Tom said. 'Bit of a walk.'

'Don't be a fuckin' idiot,' said Pete. 'Wait. I'll give you a lift.'

'Don't want one,' said Tom. 'I like to walk. Not raining any more.' He peered out through the window to see if that was true. Almost, anyway.

'Daft beggar,' said Pete. 'Don't blame me if you catch your death.' Then he laughed again. 'Listen to me. Like your mother.'

Tom's jacket slumped over a barstool; he shrugged it over his shoulders. 'Night, then,' he said. 'Thanks for the drinks.'

Pete said nothing. Sucked at his pint. Nodded.

The door of The Fisherman banged behind him. There was no echo; the sound drawn down into the dark. Through the village there were yellow streetlights, throwing their waxy pools on the road; beyond the sign where the village's name was painted, there was only black. He kept a little torch in his back pocket, but he didn't need it. He knew the ruts and curves; he walked in the dark, one foot in front of the other, his steps almost lulling him to sleep. Some time passed. Closing time at the pub came, and for a little while his back was swept and lit by the light from the cars that rushed by, the glare diffused by the thin mist that surrounded him, lowering weather, not quite rain. Pete's car. Honking, his voice shouting out of a rolled-down window, dragged away with speed. But Tom barely heard, walking, walking, his neck tucked into his collar against the mist. He was tired now. The weariness pushed through him like a kind of warmth.

When he came to a gate in a wall, a little opening, he passed through into a field. He walked more slowly, through the stubble; he'd stumbled once, long before, and twisted his ankle. Still he didn't pull out the torch. The ground rose, and then dropped, falling away towards the flat black sea. Thin streaks of light on it, spilling away from farther down the coast, orange and yellow. The red eye of a trawler in the distance; the sweep of the beam from the lighthouse on the rocks. There was no real dark any more. Maybe there never had been. But he would have liked it. True black, the black of a deep cave. You could disappear into that dark. Yes, he would have liked it.

The key was cold in his pocket. He didn't keep it on a ring, like the others, the key to the garage, the key to the van, to his padlocks – the hole for the ring was a dark eye. He felt it against his thumb as the barrel turned. The key was cold, so was the cottage, and another lamp sat on the shelf by the door; before he shut it behind him he lifted the glass, lit the wick. Shivered. Why? It was no worse in here than it was outside, but this was inside and should be warm. It only took three steps to cross to the fireplace where he'd left paper and tinder piled like a little tent, ready. He crouched down on his haunches, clicked his thumb, and the paper – scrumpled pages of Pete's *Sun* – took. Fast orange flames that hardly looked hot licked at the pale flesh of the kindling he'd split; splinters spat at him, sparked off, then burnt back towards the wood, glowing clearer now, yellow. Crack. The fire settling, taking, like his own bones relaxing with the first warmth that came. The low light threw itself on the blue and white tiles of the fire's surround, making the blurred figures appear to move. There were ships, shoes, flowerpots – but men and women too. They turned their heads to look at him. No, of course

32

they didn't. He laughed at himself. It came back at him off the end stone wall like another voice. Some company.

There were sardines in a tin with tomato sauce, a chocolate bar. He ate them sitting in front of the fire, still in his coat. He couldn't settle in this place. He was glad of it, but he couldn't settle. Not that he'd ever managed to settle anywhere. *Go on, then,* the last one said. *Run off. It's what you want to do.* She had hard eyes when she said that. Sarah. A district nurse. What was he doing with a district nurse? So he'd done as she said, and been glad to be alone here.

Or at least – that's what he'd thought, that he was alone. Now he wasn't so sure. He thought every night the fire would dispel it, the cold, the waiting cold, like a door left open. When he walked, it followed him on the road. When he woke, it blew against his cheek. Crouched here, his palms nearly in the flames, he felt it at the back of his neck blowing sweet, light: freezing too. He'd dreamt of the waves last night, the story – the waves closing over the woman's head, the green quiet after the storm, the quiet of the deep. It was never the part of that story he liked: he used to imagine the Devil, tall as the topmast, his red mouth, his sharp teeth, a tail and hooves. A trick. Only now – now he thought of the woman, of the cradle rocking, the incoming tide, the stranger, not a stranger, at the door.

CHAPTER THREE

On the motorway at eight in the morning, Janet drove with one hand while she unscrewed the top of the Thermos she gripped between her legs. 'Don't get up,' she'd said when the alarm went off. Stephen had lain quite still but she could see his eyes open and follow her around the room as she pulled on her clothes, stuffed her wash kit into the bag she'd left open by the bed.

'Won't argue any more,' he said.

They had argued. Discussed.

'If you waited – three weeks, a month? I could take some time, too. We could go up there together,' he'd said.

'I know.' Sitting after dinner, the smeared plates still in front of them, dregs of red wine in glasses, torn bread. The candle guttering.

'But you don't want to wait.'

'I don't.'

He had poured himself a little more wine; held the bottle over her glass but she'd shaken her head.

'Woman of many words,' he'd said. In the warm light of the kitchen the planes of his face were severe and composed; his hooded, almost oriental eyes. He was beautiful. As at the wedding, the first time she'd ever seen him overlaid her sight: the rustling hush of the lunchtime church, pale stone and winter sun drifting in dusty shafts, some coloured, some clear. She had not wanted to be there, not particularly. It'll be good for you, Jill had said. They're meant to be terrific. Some quartet. And there he was: his height, his intensity, his lifted bow. The moment before he began.

'What?' he'd said – to her silence.

'I don't want to wait, like I said. But thank you.'

Now she was deflecting him. Easier to confess impatience than the desire for solitude or escape. Easier to be silent, to ignore the impatience that had been mounting in her, at his watchfulness, his wish – so it seemed – to demonstrate what he was to her. He'd make her a cup of coffee and notify her he had done so. He would collect the dry cleaning and remark on his own efficiency. She was, she thought, being unfair. He was kind to make her coffee, efficient to collect the cleaning. It was right that he wished her to notice. She could move nowhere when faced with the wall of his kindness.

'You're welcome,' he'd said then, and shrugged; he knew better than to try to change her.

By late morning she was beginning to feel she was in the north, for all she was less than halfway there. She had brought the coffee but nothing to eat, and pulled off the road when she began to feel the pit of her stomach. A plate of eggs and bacon, which she devoured as if she had not eaten in a week: and in truth she hadn't, or hardly. There was too much in her head to think of any other part of her body; she had looked in the mirror and been surprised to see the same face looking back at her. Nothing had changed, not really, she knew that: and yet everything was different. She had walked out of Ernest Jackson's office into a world shifted just off its axis. She had forgotten, when she walked in the door of home, their home, that she had not thought it would be anything important.

35

'Planning permission, then?' Stephen's voice from the kitchen.

Hanging up her jacket, setting her bag down on the table. As she had thought: the bottle of wine on the counter. He had handed her a glass.

She had sat down. Told him. The same conversation, or nearly, that she'd had with Jackson, only with her in the lawyer's role.

Three weeks ago, she'd said.

But surely –

Exactly.

Yet in the following week Stephen had occasionally argued that it made no difference. She had thought her mother was dead before; perhaps she hadn't been, but as good as. Now she was. What, really, had altered?

She scraped the last rag of egg from her plate, dragged a corner of toast through bacon grease. Outside was a patch of grass, laid like a carpet and seeming to curl at the edges; an empty playground. The hard, artificial light beat down on the top of her head; the bright colours of the fast-food restaurants and shops in the service station made her squint. She brushed her teeth, bought herself a chocolate bar and bottle of water, and walked back out to the car. The wind blew hard off the road, falling away from the high sides of trucks as they hurtled north and south. She jingled the keys in her pocket and for an instant imagined hitching a lift, walking out along the slip road and standing on the shoulder, waiting, her hair blowing back, growing cold, holding out her thumb. A stranger's face in a warm cab. The thought passed through her like a current up her spine.

Of course Stephen had not wanted her to drive. She did drive; she had a licence, because the seizures had gone. Now they had returned, though she'd told him not to worry, that they would pass again. It could be this way sometimes, she'd read. No, I don't need to go to the doctor, she'd said.

'I'd rather you took the train,' he'd said.

I'd rather this; let me do that. 'I'll be fine,' she'd answered. 'I'll need a car when I'm there.'

He didn't say, You know you shouldn't be driving at all. He knew that was going too far. She had always driven; she had always lied. When she was twelve and the first seizures had come in terror and mystery and finally been given a name, the neurologist had said to her: Don't tell anyone unless you have to. He had shrugged as he said it, as if it was not something he wanted to say, but still, what can you do? There it was. He was an older man; a kindly Dane with a patch over one eye. She had learnt from her father – who was out of the room when he said those words to her, though she knew that later he had heard them also – that he had fought in a war, and she liked to imagine the loss of the eye in hand-to-hand combat. There would be snow, if he was Danish; of that her twelve-year-old self was sure. Strange how the image of the neurologist fighting in the snow with a Nazi had lingered so vividly. It was still perfectly clear to her more than two decades later.

Why? she had asked.

A twitch of the high prow of his nose. People don't like it, he said. Do not mistake me: there is nothing wrong with it. It is a condition, like any other; and a rather interesting one at that. But people have – he searched for the word. His English was very good, but perhaps Danish still came quicker. People have prejudices.

For the most part, she had done as he said. Did she think what she did was dangerous? Certainly not. Once on a dark country lane she had killed a rabbit. She had turned the corner and there was the glitter of its frozen gaze, two shining silver coins; and then a quick *thuh-bump* as the wheels went over it. She had slewed into the verge and wept, openmouthed, nose running, hiccupping. Not because she had any love for rabbits, but at the shock of this one creature's extinction, which would never have happened had she, say, stopped to fill the car's tank five minutes before, or left the dinner where she'd been slightly earlier or slightly later. She was careful; she knew, or so she thought, what was in her control. She could drive. Of course she could. The evening before she left for the north Stephen watched her put the car keys in her pocket and didn't say a word.

* * *

An ocean away, my childhood: the lights gone out. It is winter, the city's sirens have soothed me to sleep, the lights and moving figures in the apartment across the street like a bedtime story. And then waking, my father bending over me: *Janey, Janey.* My open eyes. Suddenly the dark almost absolute but for the circle and throw from the beam of a light he carries. In it I can see his smile, but I am frightened all the same. He sees it, puts his hand on my cheek. *Come on, Janey. It's okay. Get up. Let's go and look.*

I am in my pyjamas. He tells me to put my sneakers on. He finds them for me, brings them to me, and as if I were a little girl, which I think I am not any more, because I am seven, he opens their mouths and pulls out their tongues and slips them on my feet as I sit on the side of my bed. The light he has set down on the floor: it casts a diffuse yellow moon on the ceiling; the wing of the wooden seagull that hangs there catches the edge of the beam. One, two, three, four, he tightens the laces as they run through the eyelets. He ties a bow and a double knot. Come on, he says, down on his haunches, his face just below the level of mine. His young face, though it was old to me then, ancient. My father. Nothing older than that is possible, surely.

I am afraid. I don't like to say so; but he feels it when he takes my hand, perhaps a tremor, or perhaps simply the current that is always between us, the knowledge we always share because it is just the two of us. We know no one like we know each other, better than we each know ourselves, we think. *It's a blackout*, he says. *It means: the electricity is broken. But it'll get fixed. We're all right, though. We've got light.* He waves the torch around, making it seem bigger and broader, the sure sweep of a lighthouse out to sea.

A blackout. I don't think I really understand; but I believe him when he says we'll be all right. He does not lie to me. We are in this together, even in the dark. I hold tight to his hand and follow as we trace a path through our apartment, down the hall, past the heavy Spanish chest that squats by the front door, the mysteriously ugly bronze statue my father's roommate made when they were at college: I know the story because it used to frighten me, this statue, with its bulbous arms and legs that are not arms and legs. I close my eyes when we walk by it. Through the kitchen, to the fire escape; the opened window, the metal grating under my rubber soles. Up to the roof, like we do once a year, for the fireworks, only there are no fireworks tonight. There is only the quiet and the dark.

It was a spring night. I read about it years later, this blackout, and now wonder if I remember that soft air that seemed like the breath of somewhere else, not the city's grainy, iron exhalation, or if some journalist had remarked on it or even invented it. No, it's mine. Sweet warm air off the river, and only a thread of moon to limn the edges of the great stone bridge, its towers and cables, its familiar bulk less familiar with shadow heaped on shadow, no lamp out in the harbour and the spires and pinnacles of the city across the water hunkered into ghosts of themselves.

Of course, it was not silent; it can't have been. There would have been cars, headlights, honking, lit cigarettes and laughter. But I remember peace, an oasis, my father's arm around my shoulder as we stand on the roof of our apartment building and look out on to the extinguished city and in the strong dark seem to possess it. The lights have gone but we have not. My father points down at the water, the moving tide.

It doesn't notice, he says. *It still flows down to the sea.*

* * *

Farther north, the road narrowed. It still had the same name, but there were fewer cars, and instead of ploughing furrows through the land – cutting through hills, making severe, geometrical valleys – it curved around it, drawing her in, drawing her up. She had edged toward the sea, though it was not in sight, but still the sky seemed broader, paler, the horizon more distant with the prospect of open water. The earth had flattened itself; gusts slapped the side of the car and the thorn trees she could glimpse just beyond the verge were bent back with the weight of the wind.

With twenty miles to go, Janet pulled off the road into a market town. She had to cross a little bridge on which stone lions stood guard, their tails stiff as swords. The road dipped and took her through tight winding streets where

neat terraced houses shouldered up to each other as if hud-
dling for warmth. She parked in the square where the old
market had been; there were coffee shops now, a fruit and
vegetable store, a butcher, a newsagent's. Up past the end of
the square she could see a fine old building with flags hung
over its awning: a hotel. She felt for the key to the house in
her pocket. A single brass key, not unlike the key to the
London house, but its very ordinariness was peculiar to her.
Ernest Jackson had handed it to her in an envelope, along
with a little map, photocopied from a road atlas, with the
location of the house marked with a neat red x. What had
she expected? A great iron key; or perhaps something tiny,
graven gold.

There was no telling, of course, what state the house
would be in. Ernest Jackson couldn't possibly say, and
when she'd asked she saw his expression close: he knew
the limits of his business, and had built a sturdy fence at
the border – she knew right away that she'd crossed it and
stepped back. Now, with a breath of wind running down
her neck – it was colder up here than down south – she
wondered if she oughtn't to check into the hotel, just in
case. She had brought bedding with her, a duvet, sheets, a
pillow; candles and matches too. She had packed it all into
the car with a kind of abandon: it hadn't seemed real, it
was like something she had read in a book, an adventure,
a sleepover. But she was not the adventurous type. Not
that kind of adventure, anyway. She liked comfort and certainty in a place to lay her head, and now, standing out in
the early afternoon of a strange town hundreds of miles
from home, she was less sure about the sheets, the stumps
of wax that had seen service on her dining room table and
no other place, the box of matches from an expensive
restaurant.

Janet opened the boot of the car, retrieved her jacket, locked the doors. She looked at the faces of the people walking past her on the street this Saturday lunchtime: women, men, children, tracksuits, sneakers, bags from chain stores, pushchairs, hairnets, a rolled umbrella in case of rain. She could have been invisible: she wove a path through them, or they around her, and she heard their talk, their laughter – the swooping, upward curve of their voices; an optimistic accent, she decided. Janet did not consider that she herself had an accent, though of course others did; it had stuck somewhere mid-ocean and made her hard to place, which had been useful to her in the past. Now she heard her own voice in her head, set against these voices, and felt far away: no wonder they didn't see her. Their lives shot away from her in all directions, contained and complete. She was an emptiness, a mystery, at the centre. Don't be silly, she told herself. You just don't know it here. Adventure, she reminded herself, her hand shoved in her pocket, clutching the key, clutching at the memory of packing the car, of leaving, of shutting out Stephen's questions – and worse, his quiet. She turned into the door of the hotel.

It was called The White Swan. The inside was all dark wood and thick patterned carpet. The smell of hotels – never different, anywhere she went, anywhere in the country, a composite of distant bacon, furniture polish, old pipes and the faintest breath of damp – was almost a second door. She pushed herself through. There was no one at the front desk. The visitors' book was open but a fresh page had been turned and gazed blankly up at her. She rang the bell. Nothing.

'Hello?' She didn't like to ring again; though why not, she couldn't have said. 'Hello?' A little louder. Nothing. So she walked further into the building, which appeared to be entirely deserted. She passed the toilets; she passed the door to the bar; then she turned into the dining room and stopped. It was empty, still; but there was something odd about it, watery light through arched, filigreed windows. Columns which supported a ceiling that did not appear to be in need of support. Tables set with stiff white cloths, fanned napkins, heavy and scratched stainless steel, the same dark carpet, a bruised blue. But the room did not belong in this room. She could not put her finger on what was wrong.

'It's kind of spooky, isn't it?'

A voice behind her. Janet's heart jumped, and she only just stopped her body from jumping too. A pale blonde girl with hair scraped back from her face, a white blouse, black skirt, plain and sensible shoes. A little gold cross round her neck.

'Spooky?' Janet couldn't think what else to say.

The girl tapped the panelling with her finger. 'Because of the other ship. You know, the *Titanic*.' Her voice with its sing-song up-and-down.

'Sorry?' Janet was now entirely perplexed.

The girl narrowed her eyes, as if Janet had suddenly got much farther away. 'The *Titanic*? The sister ship –?'

Janet shook her head.

'Sorry,' the girl laughed. 'I thought that was why you'd come in here. It's why most people do. This dining room was from the sister ship of the *Titanic*. When they broke up the ship, they put it in here.'

Janet looked around the room again, at the pillars, the creamy windows, the gleaming wood, the tablecloths. A room holding itself in readiness for something, a room on its best behaviour, a room in a shadow no chandelier could burn off.

43

'Why?' Janet asked.

'Why what?' The girl picked at a nail, fingered her collar.

'Why put it in here?'

'Tourist attraction, I guess,' the girl said. 'I don't know. It's worked. Especially since the movie.'

If an entirely deserted hotel meant that the tourist draw had worked, Janet had no wish to think what things had been like before.

The girl seemed to collect herself then, realising that Janet had not come in just to see the dining room. 'Can I – can I help you? Do you need a room?'

Janet considered staying here in a tidy box with a kettle on the bureau, packets of long-life milk, teabags, instant coffee, a trouser press, and this room down below calling to its lost sister two and a half miles below the ocean's surface, a parallel chamber whose fine wood was made into lace by seaworms, whose iron wept rust, whose walls had watched the last smokers, the last drinkers, fight the tilt of the floor on a clear, icy night.

'No thank you,' Janet said quickly. 'Thanks very much, all the same.'

'Okay,' said the girl.

Janet tried hard not to feel that she was rising from the depths when she came back into the air, but the sensation stuck with her. She had felt the same depths coming out of Jackson's office into the street of a city she knew, where there was no echo of historic tragedy to drum against her brain – nothing except her own, and she'd never thought of that as tragedy.

She bought a watery coffee from a baker's; her Thermos had run dry a few hours back. In the car, she got out her atlas, the little map in her pocket, and compared the two. A straightforward route. And so she set off again, towards the very edge of the land where her new possession lay. The streaks of blue in the sky had disappeared; it had closed over to white now, as if she were looking up through a bowl of fine porcelain. At the perimeter of the town was the library, a little hospital, a war memorial; after that the road narrowed again and then rose over a green hill: a leap in her gut as the car crested and dipped.

Coastal route. She waited to turn, indicated, swept into a lane banked high on either side with brambles. Oncoming vehicles in middle of road, said the sign: what was she meant to do? She slowed down, craning her neck over the wheel to see farther ahead, if only a few inches; the empty feeling in her belly from the hill had not gone. She knew she was tired and she rolled down the window, listened to the road as well as watched it. It was easy to imagine, some local barrelling down a road he drove every day, hardly expecting some stranger's car . . .

She had not asked Ernest Jackson how her mother had died. Would he have known? He had volunteered almost nothing. He knew the price of information; it was his currency. He would not give it away freely, and his interests were not necessarily her own. She knew that now, and knew too that at the time, anyway, she had been far too startled to ask for detail. All the questions had come to her mind later, streaming silently out of her mouth as breath as she had turned towards home, as she had slept and dreamt and woke and walked. Now they bundled together, those questions, into a conviction: that this was how her mother had died, driving along a lane, perhaps this very lane, turning a blind corner and meeting her end: a smash of metal on metal, a black scrawl of rubber left on the Tarmac, leaking oil. The other driver: alive, in shock. She could find him. What would he know?

Janet became aware she wasn't watching the road. She pulled over on to the verge, let the car idle, dropped her head to the steering wheel, closed her eyes. She held tight to the wheel to keep her hands from shaking. She could turn back. She could forget everything she had learnt. Well, it would be easy enough to forget: she knew hardly anything at all. She had one house, she did not need another. Whatever this place was, it could go to ruin – she need not even see it, need not care, need not disrupt what was certain, what she had, what was true. There was no need.

And yet the need rose in her. The need was what made her heart beat: not only with wildness, the way it was now, but made it beat to keep her alive. With one hand she eased off the handbrake, looked in her wing mirror, and pulled back on to the lane. In the wind on her face she caught the scent of the sea.

* * *

Ruth's mother is baking a cake. I like to sit in the big kitchen of their house, their country house, which is two hours' drive out of the city and sits on a bluff overlooking the sound. It is a huge long house without a single straight line and domed skylights in every room that blink up at the sky, which is grey, just now, it is raining – *tock tock tock* goes the rain on the Plexiglas – which is why Mrs Wainewright is baking. I am nine. Ruth has been my best friend for two years. The first time I came to this house I got lost; it is all on one floor, the rooms spinning off from each other in no appreciable order. I thought of a trail of breadcrumbs; I was afraid when I woke up at night and had to pee. But now I'm not scared at all.

We are eating potato chips, watching Mrs Wainewright

pour the mix powder out of the box, add the egg, add the oil, stir with a fork, bend down to look at the oven temperature, bend again to double check. She's wearing an apron. She doesn't wear an apron very often. They have a cook. Mrs Wainewright has taken the gold rings off her fingers and has set them by the sink as she stirs. Ruth and I don't talk. That's fine.

Mrs Wainewright talks sometimes, to herself, or to the mix box, or to us, laughing at her own efforts, and we are happy to sit here in the kitchen and watch her, not doing anything, Sunday morning sliding away into lunchtime, and soon when the cake is cooled we will eat it after our tuna sandwiches and then climb back into the big station wagon and drive home to the city, listening to the radio. Ruth's little sister and brother will sit in the way back and we will ignore them.

I like it here, with Ruth, with the Wainewrights. I don't come every weekend but I come a lot. Am I invited? I never know. It just happens. And when I come I am happy, happy to be in this life which is not mine but which I know I pretend might be. What the Wainewrights give Ruth for Christmas they give me too; if Ruth gets a riding lesson, so do I. The rhythm of it is quiet and easy; there is never anything for me to be grateful for. It all just is.

Only sometimes I am – not jealous. Curious. I watch Mrs Wainewright, her long brown hair pulled back into a gold clip, her blue Lacoste shirt open at the neck, the metal band of her watch loose around her wrist, her small hands. She's pouring the batter into a pan; carefully she puts the pan in the oven and, smiling, brings the bowl over to the table so that we can run our fingers round its rim for the wet raw batter: There you go, she says, fingers crossed! Laughs. And then she pats us both on the head, running her palm down to my shoulders, to Ruth's, a slight increase of pressure from her fingers as she bends quickly to kiss the top of her daughter's head.

There is no pang, no desire in me, I am sure, for such a kiss: I can't imagine it. It is a nothing, anyway, something hardly thought of, of no importance, over as soon as done. But I remember it: a mother, a cake, a kitchen, a kiss.

* * *

'Twenty-one seventy-six,' said the man behind the counter. A petrol station with one pump that sold milk, too, and loaves of bread which Janet thought she'd have to be very hungry before she'd eat. In the fridge with the milk, sweating cheese to go with the bread. But the shopkeeper had appeared when she'd drawn in, filling her tank for her as she sat in the car with her hands in her lap, glancing at the map beside her.

She handed him the money, crumpled notes from her pocket, change. He smoothed it, took it. 'Receipt?' he said. She nodded. A grubby white shirt was stretched over his belly; cigarette smoke and the smell of petrol hung in the air. The man's fingernails were black and cracked; but he gave her what she thought might be a smile.

'A house,' she said. 'The Shieling. It's near here?'

For a second, she thought, his narrow eyes opened slightly wider. But perhaps not. 'Down the road,' he said. 'And off to the left. Can't miss it. Only house along the cliff, there.' His voice had the same up-and-down lilt as the girl's, the girl in the ship hotel.

'Right,' she said. 'Thanks.' And then she stood with her money in her hand, waiting for a beat, for two, certain he would say something else: it would be like a movie, he would warn her off, or welcome her, and she would learn the way the story was meant to go. That was how stories worked. They guided you. You followed. You didn't just walk into the fog. Unless, of course, you were making the story yourself. There were no words from his mouth; only the key, cold in her pocket against the jumble of coins.

Grey against a grey sky, a grey sea, the house. The Shieling. Down the road and off to the left, just as he said. No drive; she parked the car by a field scattered with untroubled sheep. A little path from the road, stony enough that even on the flat she could have lost her footing and turned her ankle. Darker grey slates on the roof. The window looked black, glass like a blind eye. Despite the white sheen of the sky it was bright, and she half closed her eyes against the glare and raised a hand to her brow. Five yards from the front door – green, wooden, peeling paint, an unnatural green, garish against the sea and the moss that shouldered the little stones at her feet – she stood very still. The wind blew in her ears and brushed against the voice of the sea. She could hear no human sound, even though it was the middle of the day and she knew she was not far from shops, from roads; then there was a kick and a thump, the bleat of a sheep. Something animal, at least. It was nothing to her. All of this. Until two weeks ago it had not existed. She had called it up as if it had never been and she could dismiss it again. The power was all hers.

Closer. Janet circled. She stood by the door and listened; nothing. She stood by the window and listened; nothing. She cupped her hand against her face, the edge of her palm against the cold window glass. She could see a wooden table, a chair, a narrow bed. What sent the shiver down her back that made her spin, nearly certain she would see someone behind her? She was breathing hard. The fingers of her hands spread against the rough wall for balance. Don't be ridiculous. No one there. No one, nothing. The edge of metal in her mouth. Pushing it away. Not here, not now. Metal instead in her hand. The key. The lock. A smooth turning, something falling into place.

It was cold inside, so she had walked to the fireplace. Blurred blue and white tiles, ships, Dutchmen, waves drawn as if with a child's crayon. She had reached out her hand. She had bent close to where the flames had been, and found that the ash – grey as the stone, grey as the sea, grey as the sky – was still warm.

CHAPTER FOUR

The door was open. He stopped in the path. A breeze blew up the back of his neck but he did not turn his collar up; he stood still as an animal, a stag watching from behind cover, a fox with a hound between it and its den. It was about four o'clock; the light was just beginning to fade, the grey scrim settling down over the sea, blurring the line between horizon and sky. His hands in his pockets. His palms suddenly damp. If he moved his fingers, he could feel the key cool against the pad of his thumb: had he left the door open? He never left doors open. There was no light on in the house.

He took a step, and then saw the car just behind the line of the wall. A dark green Golf, two years old, 1.6 engine, clean. A sensible car, with a little bit of power. Good nick. New tyres. The car of a careful driver. Back and forth the sea rushed and whispered, throwing guesses against the shore, hissing *who, who, who*. One step forward, then three steps back: he paced away from the cottage but always looked ahead, trusting his feet on the stony path. Whatever was waiting for him was not behind him, he knew that now.

The path rose a little at his back – he stepped slowly, his heels higher than his toes – and then it dropped down again, and he could tuck himself in the curve of the dry stone wall that bordered the field where the sheep stood and cropped at the ground, undisturbed by him, by the strange car, by the open door of the house. He heard the grass tear in their teeth, he heard the wind in the wall, the sea, he listened and watched with his ears and eyes wide. His heart beat steadily. He pulled a hand from his pocket, rested it on the cold wall. Lichen yellow and grey at the edge of his vision, rough under his fingers. He crouched down, hips, knees, ankles flexed, his head just over the level of the stone, watching.

Some time passed. Ten minutes, maybe fifteen or twenty; enough so he could sense a further diminution of the light, the turning of the earth. The air chilled now, enough so his breath made a mark of vapour like silent thought. He did not feel the cold.

Then the woman emerged from the house. The green-painted door she shut behind her. Even from this distance, he could see she held a key in her hand.

* * *

Once upon a time there was a hunter. He lived in a stone house in a forest, not far from the sea. Once, the house had belonged to his mother and his father, but they were long dead, and so the hunter lived alone.

Was he lonely? asks the boy.

The storyteller curls her arm tighter around him. *Yes,* she says. *He was lonely. Except he didn't know that he was.*

The boy looks cross. *How can you not know that you're lonely?* he asks. *You always know when you feel something.*

Well, says the woman. *Not always. You get used to things. That's how it was with the hunter. He had been alone for so long, he didn't know anything else.*

Sometimes he would go for days without speaking. He

heard the voices of the birds, the whisper of the trees, the roar of the sea. Why did he need to speak?

One day, just as the sun was about to set, the hunter walked down from his house towards the shore. He had killed a deer, and skinned it, and he thought he would wash the blood from his own skin and his knife in the salt water. The summer was nearly over, and it was not as warm as it had been. Although the fine hairs on his arms were matted down with the deer's blood, he felt them prickle and try to rise as the breeze blew over him, hinting at the cold that would soon come. He walked more quickly, to keep warm, on the path that wound a little through the wood, past birch trees and ash trees, their leaves just beginning to turn and drop.

Would he eat the deer? the boy asks. The boy has eaten chicken, and pork, which he knows is a pig, and beef, which he knows is a cow, but he has never eaten a deer. He has never thought about the blood of the animals he's eaten; he's heard stories with hunters in them before, but she has never mentioned the blood.

Yes, says the storyteller, *he'd eat the deer*. Outside his house there was a kind of rack he'd built of ash wood; some of the deer's meat he'd cut into strips to dry on the rack: you can keep it all winter that way. Some of it, he'd smoke inside his chimney. Some of it – the woman thought for a moment – he might take to the village and sell.

If there was a village, couldn't he just go there and not be lonely?

The woman laughs. *If he went to the village, it would be a different story*, she said. *Which one do you want?*

This one, says the boy.

Good, says the woman. The skin of the deer he might turn into a coat, or a rug to put over his bed and keep him warm in the winter. She pulls the quilt up over the boy's lap as she speaks. From the deer's horns he might make the handle of a knife. Nothing would go to waste. So, down he went to the sea. In the west, at the horizon, the sun was just setting, a fat, fierce ball that spilled gold on to the surface of the water and made him squint and lift a hand over his eyes. The jagged glare made it hard to see, and so it was only when he heard a strange noise that he stopped, quite still, to listen. The hunter was very good at standing still: he could wait for hours, not moving at all, in the forest. In his stillness he would become invisible, and the animals he caught would simply walk towards him, almost willing, it seemed, to be his prey. That's how he stood now, with a sound in his ears that wasn't the call of a bird, or the bark and howl of a wolf, or any noise he'd ever heard before in the wood or at sea. It was the sound of a woman singing.

* * *

The woman didn't walk towards the car. That is what he had expected her to do, but she did not do it. It had to be hers, the car – nothing else was possible, he had decided that in an instant. And in that instant, when she came out of the house, he knew too that she would walk towards the car – he could hear the sound her feet would make on the path, a light step, the gritted twist of pebble and earth under her soles – and drive away. But she did not. He crouched, so still. Shallow breaths, through his nose. An ache in his calves, in his thighs. Not moving. Watching.

Straight dark hair, pulled back in a band at her nape, the tail of it flicked over the collar of her waxed coat, a coat that had been bought and worn in a town. A high forehead, pale, a pale face and a tired face, he could tell that even at this distance. He could tell she was tired from the way she stood, too, a little hunched, as if she were colder than the weather really merited. He almost expected her to shake. When she had pulled the door to behind her she had shoved her hands in the slit pockets of her coat and stared ahead, unseeing, he thought, though her eyes would have been set on the inland road, the hedge, the hill, the lip of the darkening sky. The sea at her back, the house at her back. Jeans, boots. Points of light in her ears; little stones, something precious, something she always carried with her. A thin drift of knowledge misted over to him; he caught its scent. She turned her head towards the car, her neat chin and straight nose in profile. Still, she didn't see him. Her eyes looked inside. Then she turned her head the other way, and her body too, and began to walk along the path that led down to the sea.

It cut and dipped, first into dune, then down towards the flattening shelves of whale-grey rock lapped at last by the water's edge. He stood up then, and followed behind, trying to match each step to hers so she would hear nothing but her own footsteps. She moved down on the stone shelf – hard rock, but mud once, he knew that. Not so long ago the footprint of a dinosaur had been found when the tide went out, a single great, splayed foot as if the creature had made some tremendous hop into the water. Where was the other print? Worn away by the sea, he supposed. Now the woman made her way down towards the water; she had taken her hands out of her pockets for balance. They were ringless, the fingers spread out as if they caught the air and held her steady, and she did move steadily, not hesitant, along and up and down the rock as it buckled away from the hills, stepping around the hollows where pools of green water collected, stone cups filled with slick weed and limpets.

He stayed just above her. She moved right to the edge of the water – taking a quick step back when the tide, which was high, made a quicker rush forward and nearly lapped against her toes. The key in his pocket; the key in hers. He could feel the magnetic pull between them – these two inanimate metal objects, though to him nothing made of metal could quite be so described. The eye of the key, its teeth, its brightness. The key longs for the lock; the lock waits to be opened. The lock can be picked, its heart fooled by whispers and pins. But her key was true: it must be. In the pocket of her jeans it would lie now, against her thigh, warmed by her skin through the cloth.

He watched her back and felt his own heart turning like the heart of a lock.

She was a stranger. He knew nothing. He knew all that he needed to know.

A movement of her head, sudden. He flinched, thinking she would turn and see him, but she did not: it was something in the water she had seen, and he could trace the direction of her gaze. The water was dull under the dull sky, slatey and forbidding, the colour of the north, and dashed with scraps and tatters of white where it broke against itself or against the rocks under the surface. But there it was: grey against the grey, the curve of a dappled, whiskered head with wide onyx eyes.

The woman made a sound. The wind brought it back to him: a little cry, or the beginning of a laugh. He couldn't tell, and then her bare hand in front of her mouth as if her noise would frighten it away. Not it: them – two seals now, one just behind the other. They stood in the water as the pair of humans stood on the shore, and for a moment he thought she would see it as he did, and turn. But still she watched, and her back had straightened, she was up on her toes, weariness dropped away from her like a cloak she'd let fall from her shoulders. If he could have seen her face, her mouth would be smiling, her eyes too, he was certain of it.

Maybe she'd never seen one before, a seal, or only in a zoo. Here they were everywhere, a plague on the fishermen, lolling insolently on the rocks of the little offshore islands: some of the trawlers had given up their nets and gone over to the side of the seals, running sightseeing tours from the little harbour town. The quayside there used to sparkle with the scales of the fish the boats brought in, cast-off stars ground into the concrete and wooden pilings: now the lobster creels and nets were stacked decoratively by placards offering trips to the rocks, the seals, to the stump of the old lighthouse that poked its stone thumb out of the water.

He'd gone out once, at the beginning of the summer. All the money he had in his pocket that day, a glowing day of high white cloud and indigo water: he'd wanted to feel the sea under his feet. He'd walked past the big shed that housed the blue and orange lifeboat; toy boats, he always thought the lifeboats looked like, bulbous and gleaming to trick the sea. He peered in the door of the building as he passed. Toy or not, it looked imprisoned, dragged up on land, hemmed in by the walls of its housing. He walked faster, down to where the tourists in brightly coloured anoraks and brand-new walking boots were already eating ice creams, fat swirls of snowblind white, not that long past breakfast time. He put his money on the first of the little stalls he came to: it was blue-painted, clumsily decorated with seashells and rope and startled-looking, elliptical fish. There was a young woman behind the counter who had the look about her of someone's hard-pressed sister. He had to scrabble to make the money with change. Seagulls squealed and dived for squashed and greying chips on the sea wall; the sister-girl looked at her watch. 'Boat leaves in ten minutes,' she said. 'Down there,' and pointed down toward the steep concrete steps that led from the harbour to the water.

Gypsy, the boat was called. It was red and white painted, plastic chairs bolted to the open deck and benches inside, foam covered with slick vinyl patched with duct tape. Black tears of water sloshing in the grooved metal of the deck. He sat in the uncomfortable chair on the boat's starboard side, gazing down at the sea closed in the arms of the harbour, its surface swirled with rainbows of diesel and oil, littered with flotsam: chip wrappers, lolly sticks, scraps of sodden wood and floating plastic twine, pale green, bright pink. When the engine kicked into life with a blue belch he felt better, less agitated, and when they pulled out of the harbour he'd lifted his face into the wind and shut his eyes, shutting out too the nasal voice of the captain – he supposed it was the captain – leaking out of the tinny speakers chained to the rails, describing the coast, the sea, the castles north and south, their long-dead feuds and vanished kings, the famous rescue from the lighthouse on a black long night generations ago when the sea looked for souls to pull to its breast – no, he wasn't listening to the captain, though he heard what was said. He did listen when the recounting began of the tonnage of fish, the price of the catch, the change in the market: he heard anger there, and his ears pricked up.

Already the clouds had begun to scud across the sky, obscuring the morning: brightness wouldn't last. The boat skipped in the water, smacking down hard when it turned for the rocky islands. A little boy of about six, sitting on his father's knee – the only other passengers on the deck – shrieked with delight as a fan of spray pattered over his face. The father grimaced and smeared his glasses with his sleeve.

The seals were sprawled on the island's rocks, thick tapering cylinders of fur, sleek, grey, white, black. They twisted their bodies to catch the shafts of sun that broke through the gathering cloud: when the boat approached, some tumbled into the water and slid underneath the surface. He leant his chin on the cold metal rail for a closer look. Some of them, less timid or maybe older and more used to the run of the tourist boats, didn't flinch from the diesel's noise but lifted their heads instead, looked up and straight at the boat as if curious about these visitors. One, it seemed to Tom, followed his gaze particularly, turned its head as the boat moved – much more slowly now, for the view of the seals – and when its fathomless black eye blinked he felt a prickle at the back of his neck. He laughed, loud, which made the father of the boy glance at him and then glance away.

He remembered it now, that day out at the seal rocks. That rise in his skin, something brushing past, not quite recognised. Here it was again, that inkling, connected to the woman, connected to the seals, a link he wouldn't be able to name but that ran through the marrow of him. He waited for her to turn. She would turn.

*　*　*

Now that the hunter heard, he could also see, the woman says. The boy settles himself tighter against her side. They are sitting together on his bed, a bed in another strange new house. He doesn't like this house much – down a narrow

59

street where the other houses press too close, where there is always someone coming or going and you can hear the people next door and wonder if they can hear you. He tries to keep quiet, because of that. He climbs up the stairs softly, and shuts the door of his room softly: he makes it like a game. He is a spy. No one will catch him. At night, though, when she sits beside him and tells him stories, he can believe that everything is the same as it has ever been, what he'd imagined it had once been. At night, there is no new house, there is no street, there are no neighbours. There is only her voice and the story.

Now that the hunter heard, he could also see, the woman says. He moved away, just a little, walking backwards, heel and toe, until he could hide himself behind the broad trunk of an oak. The woman was standing right at the edge of the water, silhouetted by the crimson sun, her feet lapped by the gentle tide. She had a comb in her hand – he couldn't quite make it out, but it must be – and she was drawing it through her dark hair. She tugged at the ends, and as he watched her he suddenly recalled his mother, how she would sit on the bed and do the same, combing and unknotting her hair before she wove it with swift fingers into a braid. Sometimes the woman broke off her song when she came to a particularly stubborn knot: the breeze carried her voice to him as he stood behind the oak, and he could hear, it seemed, her every breath. The song had no words he could make out, but was a pretty, simple tune, rising and falling with the drowsy calm of a lullaby.

After a little while, when the sun's edge had fallen just below the flat rim of the sea, her strokes became smoother: the knots had gone. Her pale arm rose and fell, rose and fell, and he could see now too that she wore nothing but her skin. Still he did not move. He did not speak or call out. He watched, as he always did, waiting to see what would come, what would happen next.

The woman at the shore threw her thick hair over her shoulder; it reached nearly to her waist. Then she walked, with long sure strides, to the uneven shelf of rocks that rose up from the shingle there. It was an expanse of fissured stone, hard to tell, the hunter had always thought, if they were many stones worn so they lay close alongside each other, or a single stone broken up by deep cracks. She laid the comb down on the flat of the rock and then reached down to one of the cracks and tugged – with much the same gesture as she'd used to pull at her hair – and drew out from the breach an animal skin.

It was nothing like the hide he'd taken from the deer. That was rough, pale brown, speckled: this was smooth, dark as her hair, heavy with wet. When she'd gathered it into the crook of her arm, she bent to tuck the comb into the opening where the pelt had been; then she shook it out and held it away from her, examining it, and once again the hunter remembered his mother, how she would hold one of his shirts against the light to see where it needed mending, narrowing her eyes so her gaze was as sharp as the pins in her sewing basket. The woman drew the skin close to her, right against her breast.

Maybe it was then he looked away. He must have looked away, because first she was there and then she was not, and where she had been there was a seal on the rock, a dark slender beast with smooth wet fur and a round black eye. With a swift, liquid undulation that echoed the curl of the waves, it flowed down the shelving stone and – before the hunter could blink twice – slipped away into the sea.

For a long time the hunter didn't move. The sun sank

away into the sea, almost as the seal had done; the evening star hung in the violet sky, but the moon was new and dark. It grew colder. Only when the hunter knew he would begin to shiver did he step away from the tree, out from behind it, and not back towards his house but straight to the shelf of rock. He knelt, and reached down as the woman had for her skin, and found her comb where she'd left it. He held it in his hand and peered at it in the dusk; it was made of bone, with the teeth at one end fine and at the other broad. He was a man who made things with his hands and he knew this was well-made, smoothed on every surface.

The sea was calm, and nothing broke through its rippling skin. A gull veered into view, dipping a wing, wheeling on the balance of the air, its watching eye invisible in its black head. The hunter held tight the comb and stood. He began to walk back up the beach, to the path that led through the green forest where the night animals were just beginning to wake. He had forgotten to dip his arms, his knife, in the sea: as the comb warmed in the palm of his hand the blood of the deer became sticky again and marked the polished bone, the little, fine sharp teeth.

* * *

The woman stood for longer than he thought she would. The seals had ducked their heads back under the water, back to their business beneath the waves. When they'd disappeared he'd seen her flinch a little and then rise up again on her toes, looking out hard at where they'd been, hoping they'd come back. They, however, had seen enough. But she stood in the fading light, her hands back in her pockets, waiting, waiting for something.

When she turned, she didn't see him. So he began to walk

towards her, and as soon as he did she heard his footsteps and stopped in her tracks, because – he was aware – she had been in a place where she knew there was no one, even though she had been inside the house and seen what she had, his few things, but there had been no other car, and no sound to tell that anyone had arrived. She stopped, but he kept walking until he was close enough to see the colour of her eyes. She wanted to back away. There was nowhere to go but the sea.

'Afternoon,' he said. He thought of saying, hello, but then thought he would greet her as one walker on a path – meeting by chance – would greet another. A remark on the time of day.

'Afternoon,' she said too, her eyes glancing over his shoulder to see if there was anyone else, looking left and right as if this were an ambush. Her feet were planted wide apart in their tight-laced boots. He was blocking the path. If she wanted to return to her car she'd have to go past him.

'You saw the seals,' he said. She nodded, a dip of her chin. 'The fishermen hate them. They get all the catch. They can open the pots, get the lobsters and crabs.' She looked straight at him. 'Maybe they're just smarter than the fishermen.'

'Maybe,' she said.

'You visiting here? Lovely part of the world.'

He could see that her hands were balled into fists in her pockets. He was too close to her. She lived in the city, where degrees of proximity were carefully maintained, but she had no bearings here, and could not judge what his nearness meant.

'Yes,' she said, 'I –' and she stopped, because even though he was a stranger, it is hard to tell a lie, and perhaps harder to lie, though one could never know, to one who knows more than you think. 'Yes, I'm visiting.'

'Staying at the hotel in the village?'

'Yes.'

He smiled then. 'I don't think you are,' he said.

'What?' Now her mouth set itself in a straight line.

'I said, I don't think you are. And I don't think you're visiting.'

She moved then, straight at him, but when she went to walk around him towards her car he simply took a step sideways and blocked her path again.

'Excuse me.' Her voice breaking on the first vowel.

'I'm not going to hurt you,' he said.

'Really,' she answered, her voice expressionless.

'I'm sorry. Really.' He spread out his hands, to show they were empty, to show he had made some kind of mistake. 'But I know you've been in the house.' He turned his gaze toward it, the house, for an instant.

Her dark eyes with their fine brows widened. She took a breath. 'Congratulations. You've been watching me.'

'Not for so long. But a little bit, yes. I saw your car. No one comes here, much. And when I tried the door, it was open. It's never open. I don't leave it that way.'

'You – you don't – what?'

'Leave the door open.' He reached down into the pocket of his jeans and pulled out the key. He held it up in front of her, not speaking, and then she too reached down into her pocket and pulled out a key. Soon the sky would begin to darken; the wind had picked up, raising white rips on the water. The marram grass flattened itself against the dune. She flinched a little when he took it from her fingers, the key, but then she moved closer to him when he took them both and laid them together, flat against the skin of his palm, head to head and tail to tail, the pattern of the brass teeth matching exactly. She looked down at his open hand and then up, into his face.

'Welcome home,' he said.

* * *

Every night for a month, the hunter returned to the shore with the bone comb in his pocket. His wish to see the seal-woman again took him away from the forest and made him less patient than he had been. His aim was not as true, and sometimes he found that the image of the seal-woman in his mind made it hard to see what was in front of his eyes.

So – says the boy –

Yes?

So, he was lonely?

Well, yes. Or he was in love.

The boy considers this, twirling the edge of the quilt between his fingers. He looks up. *I love you*, he says.

I love you, too, says the woman, smiling. *Should I go on?*

The boy nods, and leans his head against her.

Every night the hunter returned to the shore, but every night he had only himself for company. He watched the surface of the water; sometimes, thinking she might be able to see him before he could have seen her, he hid behind the oak that had given him shelter that first night. He watched the sun sink; the stars appeared, blossoming silver against the silk sky. Only when it was too dark to see would he turn his back to the water and head for home. Sometimes, he discovered, he'd forgotten to leave the fire banked, and the house would be cold. He would lie in his bed, wrapped in animal skins, wide awake but dreaming of the seal-woman, the rise and fall of her long arms, the tilt of her dark head, her feet caressed by the sea.

Then one night, she came. The hunter had nearly given up hope; or perhaps he simply didn't remember what hope felt like. Only a month since he'd seen her, the seal-woman; but his life before that evening seemed to belong to someone else. He was behind the oak, leaning with his palms flat against the rough bark, his boots buried in the browning leaves that were falling faster now. Then he heard a splash, not the sound of the waves on the shore but the sound of the water opening: and then there it was, there she was, the seal, pulling herself up out of the sea and on to the surface of the rock.

Again he wondered if he'd looked away, her transformation was so swift. A shadow passed over her, he might have said; there was a shimmer in the air like midsummer heat, and yet it was the cool of the evening. The shimmer passed and she stood on the stone shelf in her white human skin, the heap of her sealskin at her feet. She stepped down from the ledge and for a little while she walked back and forth at the edge of the water, on the wet stones –

They didn't hurt her feet? asks the boy.

What?

The stones. When you walk on stones at the beach, it hurts your feet.

Not her feet: because she was really a seal, she didn't mind the stones.

Oh, says the boy. But the storyteller doesn't continue, because she can see that he's thinking. *So: was she really a seal or really a lady?*

The storyteller pushes her fingers through his hair, kisses it.

She walked back and forth at the edge of the water, on the wet stones, and then after a while she turned her back to the sea, although she seemed to do so with great effort.

The hunter could see her face now, more clearly. She was not beautiful. Her mouth was wide and her nose looked like someone had broken it, once. Her eyes were very dark. The hunter made himself as narrow as he could, shifting a little behind the tree, summoning up all his animal cunning as she made to go towards the path.

But she never got near him. Halfway up the beach she stopped, very suddenly, almost falling, as if someone had tied a rope around her waist and pulled. She turned quickly then, running back to the water's edge until her feet were in the waves. He watched the long arc of her spine as she went, her shoulders rising and falling with her quick panting breaths; she dropped down on to her knees so that her hands were in the water too, leaning forward on her arms, her hair falling into the licking foam and trailing back and forth with the ebb and flow like seaweed. Then she stood, flicking the wet ends of her hair over her back, and walked back to the ledge for her comb.

She knelt again, on the rock, reaching into the crevice. The hunter took the comb out of his pocket and held it in his hand, tight, so that the teeth dug into his palm. She felt in the rock, and felt again, moving both hands into the stone and peering into the shadowy gap. Then, empty-handed, she sat back on her haunches, her back to the water again, and looked, it seemed, straight at him: and so he stepped out from behind the tree. Her gaze travelled out to him and his to her and he felt his heart tighten, as if a knot had been pulled, and the breath left his body in a sigh. He took a step toward her – they were ten yards apart – and held out the comb, reaching out his arm with his palm towards the sky. But she did not move to take it. She made no sound, but quick as running water stooped to gather the skin at her feet, lifting it, unfolding it, and somehow wrapping herself in it so once again she was lost to him, becoming her seal-self, tumbling back into the waves, which opened for her and closed again over her head.

The hunter shouted out – no words, only a cry – and ran right to the edge of the water, his boots gathered in the salt. He wanted a name in his mouth, but he had nothing, only the coarse sound of his longing. The stars glared down at him, bitterly bright in the rushing dark, and he held the bone comb out towards the horizon, calling, calling, calling.

The sound of the boy's breathing, in rhythm with her voice. He's so sleepy, leaning against her: is he even listening? The slight pressure of his body against hers, its small weight. Still, she speaks, her voice low and even. His eyes are open, wide in the dark.

He knew she would come back at the new moon. So that night, the night when there would be only stars alive in the sky, he walked back down to the strand. He didn't bring the comb; he left it, where he always kept it now, set above the fire, white against the dark grey stone.

He waited. He wished to become trees and rocks and sea. And so it was, as she rose from the foam. The shapely seal-head first, the long body, and then her body as she became herself, the starlight on her flank as she stepped with human feet through the rolling scrim of surf, shaking out her hair, combless, dragging her fingers through it and hypnotised, it seemed, by the land, her swift seal-soul abandoned with her skin.

He tracked her. He knew how to do that. He paced down the beach. She had her back turned to him, and she had begun to sing, not a song he had ever heard or even wished to hear, but it entered him like a blade until he bled the music out. Her voice was high and shrill and not beautiful at all, but it was everything she was. Against the tide of her song he moved towards his goal, the little heaped rag on the rock, her cloak of self. Closer he came, and closer.

How did she not hear? Perhaps she had no wish to hear. Perhaps she knew her fate. She kept singing, singing, as the hunter set his bootsole on the stone and then felt the soft gathers of fur and flesh in his hands, flowing through his fingers, breathing the sharp salt animal stink of it, the scent running down into his mouth, over his tongue, filling his lungs. It was only when he turned and ran that she heard, her song devoured by a shriek. He ran up into the woods he knew even in darkness, faultlessly skipping to the blind of a great tree, a hiding place, stuffing the skin down into the throat of the wood.

The noise she made was like something being ripped apart, keening and wordless, harsh, the voice of the storm. And yet he ran down to it, he did not want to run away, he clattered back down through leaves and branches, on to the grinding rocks to where she knelt at the edge of the sand, sand thickening the skeins of her still-wet hair, sand frosting her thighs and arms. Her head tipped back, the bow of her throat like something laid back for the knife. He stopped. She silenced herself, and stared.

The boy is asleep now. That's good. The woman slips off the bed and pulls his body down so he lies as he should, his head on the pillow, and she smooths the quilt over his body. His hair is moist with the heat of his sleep; she pushes it back behind the whorled shell of his ear and kisses his temple. Then she kneels by the bed. Her voice is a whisper.

When the seal-woman tried to step on the earth she cried out in her wordless language; as far as the hunter could tell, it was as if she had been burnt, or cut. When she had stared

69

at him he had dropped to the sand, kneeling as she knelt, looking right into her dark eyes in the darkness, her broken face, the open wonder of her mouth. He took her hand – it was freezing cold, as cold as a stone drawn from the sea – and simply put it against his heart. Then he rose, and with his arms under hers lifted her as lightly as if she were a child, or something he'd killed in the woods. That night in his bed she gasped as she felt for the first time the rough skins of deer and bear he kept heaped to sleep in; but then she made a noise that might have been a laugh. The hunter stretched his body out in the chair by the fire to sleep. He thought he would watch her, but he was tired, and soon the only eyes open in the long black of the new moon night were hers.

* * *

She followed him. He knew she would. He turned his back and set his tread along the path and heard her behind him, falling in step. The light was beginning to crawl back, the sky to darken; he noticed rubbish along the path, stooped to pick it up – a gum wrapper, the shred of a crisp packet faded, blown from somewhere – he didn't break his step as he bent, balled them, shoved them in his pocket. Like he owned the place, which he did. Putting his palm flat against the door, the rough flakes of paint. He pushed against it, opened it, let them in.

She stood still while he lit the lamp. He had turned to her, though he did not look at her. Her face in the shadow, but he could sense her gaze, the rigidity of it, the intensity. Whatever she was expecting, it had not been this. Whatever he had been expecting – no, it had not been this. His hands did not shake. The yellow light lapped up from the wick, breathing air like a human. A glass bowl full of light, set on the shelf.

'Get out of my house,' she said.

He smiled. He could not help it. The little flame set in the dark of her eye.

'Get out of my house.' She was not smiling.

'Why don't we have a drink?' he said. On the mantel there was a bottle of good whisky; there were two glasses, unmatched, cheap tumblers. He'd taken them from the pub. He stepped over to the ashy fireplace to retrieve it all, the bottle uncorked, the bronzy smell of the malt.

'I don't want a drink,' she said. 'I want you to get out of my house. This is my house. I have papers to prove it. I don't know how you got in here, how you have a key, but if you just go now I won't say anything about it. Now, please go.'

Please. He liked please. He poured two generous shots and reached one out to her. She didn't move. How curious she'd looked, how alert, watching the seals; now she was coiled and tight. 'Possession is nine-tenths of the law, they say, don't they?'

'I'll call the police.'

He took a sip of whisky. He was not unafraid. 'There's no phone here.'

It was nearly pity in her face. 'I have a phone,' she said. Her voice was odd; he couldn't place it. Flattened and almost harsh.

'Right,' he said. 'Of course.'

They stood facing each other. 'Aren't you curious?' he asked.

'No. Get out.'

'Liar. Of course you're curious. I have a key. You have a key. How did you get a key? I want to know. Have a drink.

71

I'll light the fire. I could find us something to eat. Nothing much. Bread, some cheese. A tin of something. You look hungry.'

He made his voice easy and light, so it would float over her like a veil. She brushed it aside. 'I am telling you,' she said, 'to leave. I am not asking you. This is private property. It is my property. I am not going to say it again. You will leave now. Don't pick up anything, don't take anything, I don't care what all of yours is here. Go. Go.'

Her chin lifted and her arms straight at her sides. She was hard to gauge. He felt her poise and containment. He liked them, her low, steady words. She had worked to keep them from breaking, he guessed.

Later he would wonder if it was simply his smile, he had not meant to smile, that had pierced her calm. For he was calm when he said, 'And I am telling you that I am not going. You don't know that this isn't my place as much as it is yours. I want to know why you came here. I'm asking you for a simple thing. I am not leaving. That's all there is. You can't make me leave. I wonder how you would try.' He took a step nearer to her, pushing at the air between them, compressing it with threat. He knew his own strength and risked a release of her fear.

And yet he didn't expect her to run at him; he had missed that, whatever the signal had been. He was caught off balance, leaning on his back foot, and then her hands were on his neck, his shoulders, pushing him or clutching him, and she cried out. The glass fell from his hand and smashed on the stone flags; the whisky wet his chest. He grabbed at her, her wild arms, finally finding her wrists and holding hard, pulling her down until she cried out again, a different sound – and her knees bent and as she fell he released her but saw her hand stretch out towards the stone, towards the broken glass.

Then she was sitting, holding her own hand, her eyes open very wide, the pool of blood in her palm. Her chest rose and fell, quickly.

'You'll be all right,' he said. He straightened. 'Come here.' He reached down for her. He thought she would refuse him. She almost put her right hand down on the stone to raise herself, but the scatter of glass stopped her, and she let him pull her to her feet, his hand on the inside of her arm. Her left hand held up, its vibration, a thick drop falling through her fingers and plashing on the floor, he heard it. He stepped behind her quickly and slipped her coat from her shoulders, throwing it over the table; then he led her into the little scullery, where a deep stone sink sat beneath a low window of small, thick panes of cloudy glass. He left her at the sink while he fetched the lamp, and then ran water, which came freezing from the tap in sputtering gouts. She held her hand in the water so the blood from the cut – at the base of her palm, beside her thumb – thinned and swirled down the drain. He watched it pulse out from her, its steadiness and life. She didn't resist when he took her hand in his, turned it a little in the waterflow to see, holding the lamp in his other hand.

'Not so bad. I've seen worse.'

'I need to sit down,' she said. She was trying to keep her voice steady.

'Of course.'

From a neat pile below the sink he took a clean teacloth, folded it thickly and gave it to her. 'Press,' he said, and she did.

He carried the lamp back to the table where there were two chairs; he guided her with his touch an inch from her ribcage, pushing against a cushion of air. He left her with

73

the lamp, returned to the scullery, came back with a tin box that he set on the table and opened, pulling out gauze, tape, antiseptic cream.

'Here,' he said, 'Give me your hand.' So she held it out, her hand to him, and he lifted off the towel and inspected the cut, which was clean and not too much more than a couple of centimetres long. The smell of the cream was not so unlike the smell of the whisky drying on his shirt; he tore open a white gauze pad and laid it on the wound, and then drew out a length of sticky white tape to fix it. In order for it not to slip he had to wrap the tape around her wrist and through her middle fingers, making her a gauntlet. When he had finished, he took her other hand and lifted it to set one palm against the other, the whole against the cut. 'Press again,' he said.

She sat with her elbows on the table, her palms together as if in prayer. He moved around her, fetching a dustpan and brush, sweeping the glass, collecting its fragments; he could feel her eyes on his back when he turned away from her.

When he was sure there were no more glass splinters on the stone, he began to lay the fire. Newsprint, kindling, coarser wood. The scrape and catch of the lit match and the rising flame; as it lifted towards the chimney and began to give its light to the room, he saw her turn towards it. How can a human not turn towards a fire? He crouched down, blew, tasting the smoke, the heat at his face, the cooler air at the back of his neck, her gaze, her gaze.

The whisky bottle was still on the table. So was her glass, untouched. He rose and fetched a mug from the scullery, a chipped teacup laced with painted blue leaves. When he moved to sit down beside her he looked into her eyes, almost wondering if she'd try again, kick out the chair from under him – but she only held him with her stare, her back stiff, her hands still held together. He poured the whisky into the teacup, lifted it to his lips, felt it heat his mouth and numb his tongue.

Then she looked away and sighed, the slope of her back changing to rest against the frame of the chair. Outside, the bruised sky was beginning to close down on itself and the sea poured its language into the sand. She had resigned herself to something; so had he. Unclasping her hands, she took up the unbroken glass of whisky and drank. She looked at him, her eyes a wall, her thoughts invisible.

'I'm not a thief,' he said.

CHAPTER FIVE

So Janet sat at the table – his table, except that it couldn't be his – in the dark which was beginning to pull itself around the walls of the house. The sea merged with the sky, grey leaking into a thread of mauve at what could barely be discerned, through the window glass, as the horizon; it was as if Earth, air and water were cupped in a bowl. She kept her palms pressed together, as he had told her; she let her gaze travel from the window to the lamp and rest on its flame until, when she looked away, there was a dark spot in her vision where the light had overwhelmed her eye.

His movements were quick and sure as he bent to sweep the glass from the floor with a pan and a brush he'd fetched from the little scullery. The steel lip of the pan scraped against the flags of the floor; she moved her legs as he reached to brush beneath the table, the fragments of glass clicking like beads as they were gathered up. Back to the scullery, the rain of splinters and dust into the bin; and then she kept her back to him, not moving, but heard him begin to light the fire where she had felt the warmth from last night's embers: paper, the crack of breaking kindling, the little roar of the first flame.

She should have turned to face him, because she was afraid of him; but she was afraid too to show that, to give him anything at all. His touch, when he had bound her opened palm, had been gentle – a contradiction, for she felt in the pressure of his fingers no wish to harm her, and yet in her mind was the certainty that he would. Holding her wrist, spreading her fingers so the tape could pass between them, sealing the wound. She had never had stitches, not once in her life; she had been lucky. He had told her she would not now; but why should she believe him? He might let her bleed to death here, in her own house. Her own house. She felt warmth between her palms and peered in. The blood was beginning to soak through the gauze.

She heard the fire take; then, she turned. Shadows in his deep-set eyes, orange light on his curious, pale halo of hair that was thickened with wind or salt. He looked at the fire, not back at her, leaning into it and breathing in its heat, breathing out its life. He crouched, his heels raised; stood, got another cup from the kitchen, poured the whisky – the bottle was still open on the table – sat, and drank, and so did she.

'I'm not a thief,' he said.

When she'd parted her hands to pick up the glass, there was a smear of blood on her unhurt palm, transferred from the leaking gauze. 'It'll clot up,' was the next thing he said. 'Don't worry.'

What did he sound like? Even after all this time, she was not good at that; from the north, certainly, but from where she couldn't place. Would she know the sounds they made, here? She would not, though she tried to recall the voice of the man in the petrol station; that did not help.

Janet looked around the single room. It was hardly a house, this; it was a shelter, solid, but a shelter all the same. How long had he been here? It was impossible to tell. It smelled clean, and aired. She had thought that the place – whatever it was – would be shut up, dead, powdered with dust and hung with cobwebs and spiderwebs. Unwelcoming. But this, in its spareness, was not welcoming either. The sticks of furniture, only the table and chairs, the bare bed, a white mirrored dresser the only hint of something decorative – there was nothing to grasp. The mantel over the tiled fireplace bare, except for a candlestump and a metal . . . mask, she would have said, Aztec in its ferocity, but blank and forbidding. She had been imagining taking possession of her property in the usual way – wiping, polishing, washing, scrubbing, buying a broom, finding old rags, digging out grease, up to her elbows in rubber and soap. That would have given her time to think and, she was convinced, would have taught her something about how and why she had been left this place. She would have been able to discover (on her hands and knees, her head under a sink) what it might mean, her legacy, and what she could learn.

But here he was, an orderly stranger who'd stood in her way, stolen her house, bandaged her hand and poured her a drink. Who said he was not a thief but had a thief's closed and unreadable face.

'I don't believe you,' she said finally. 'I don't believe anything you've said.'

'Why don't you go?' he asked. 'You'll be fine to drive. You could go back to the town. Or I could drive you there. I don't mind walking back.'

'There isn't a car here.'

'In your car, I meant.'

She laughed. 'I don't think so,' she said.

'Are you hungry?'

'Yes,' she said. 'I am.'

'Good,' he said. 'So am I.'

* * *

Of course I ask my father for stories. My favourite is how they met, he and my mother, because in it there are ships, and icy cold, and the possibility that none of this would have happened at all, and so I would never have existed. Chance. Grace, my father calls it, not chance – a kind of gift. It can be very simple: why Ruth had moved from another school and so was available to be my best friend. What if she hadn't left that other school? Would someone else be my best friend? Would I have somehow found Ruth anyway? That seems very unlikely. My friends are my friends from school. It is hard to imagine Ruth, walking around in another part of the city with a different friend. I know this ought to mean I'd have a different friend too, but somehow this is harder to reckon with: I usually end up by thinking that this change of chance, or Grace, would mean I'd have no friends at all. Grace can take as well as give. Grace had taken my mother. That's how Grace works. You can't know what she'll do.

My father tucks me up in bed. Maybe it is winter, and the heating whirrs comfortingly. I like the sound, and will turn it on again in the night if I wake up and find it's turned itself off: the room will get too hot. I am, perhaps, eight, but this can be any night in any number of years. A little humidifier breathes steam to counter the dryness. DeVilbiss is the brand, I will always remember that later, years later: why should that be when so much else goes? DeVilbiss, and I've covered it with stickers I trade in class. I have a sticker book with leaves made from waxed paper so the stickers can be peeled off, restuck, stuck again. Night.

Tell me about the ship, I say. How you went on the ship. I have seen ships like the one he went on in the harbour, the big liners, but I haven't been on one myself and they scare me a little. I think of ships and I think of shipwrecks, though I don't think of airplanes and plane crashes.

So he tells me. His voice is clear in my head, though it's less his voice than the images his voice makes, which are so distinct to me it's as if I were there myself. He was an architecture student – he was twenty, at college, a boy, a boy so much younger than I am now, an American boy with American parents. No one in his family had ever been to Europe, not, at least, since someone must have come from there generations ago – but theirs wasn't a family interested in that kind of history. He'd worked nights in a bar up by the school to save for his fare; it was a place on the wide avenue where his professors would come sometimes for beers. Pouring beer, he tells me, was mostly what he did on those nights, but he bought himself a book (he didn't really have the money but he told himself it was an investment) and learnt to mix drinks. I like to make him say their names, even though I can't imagine the taste of them. They wouldn't taste nice, I know that, but the taste of the words in his mouth and then – whispered back – in mine is like the taste of neon, or mink. Gibson, Martini, Manhattan, Singapore Sling, Whiskey Sour. Some drinks had maraschino cherries in them; I like those. We have a jar in the fridge.

So he'd saved his money, but it wasn't enough. His father – whose drugstore nearly went belly-up in the Depression, my grandfather whom I never met – gave him two hundred dollars. I'd never been so surprised by anything, my father says. The ship was named after a queen; it was June when he sailed, on the afternoon tide. Passengers pressed close against the rail and – it was just like in the films – waved their handkerchiefs and the crowd on the quay waved their handkerchiefs back. Some people had confetti, and little party horns. No one had come to see my father off. He was alone, but he didn't mind that, he says.

You weren't lonely? I ask.

Just because you're alone doesn't mean you have to be lonely, he says. You can be your own good company, you know that. The pleasure of solitude.

Solitude. This is a new word.

Maybe I was a little lonely, but I liked that, he says. I was with people all the time, at school, when I was working, with my family, I knew everyone all the time. Now I was going where I didn't know anyone and I could be anything I wanted. It was like being in a story, a story I was making up every day. You understand? I nod.

It took nearly a week to cross the sea. A whole ocean! Mostly the weather was fine and he would stand at the rail, watching the blue-black water slide by, or the ship slide by the water: you could become hypnotised wondering which was which. He was travelling third class, sharing his windowless cabin with a nearly silent Pole who just once showed my father black and white photographs of his family, a woman and a little boy. It was impossible to tell, my father says, how old the photographs were; and possible to wonder if these people were still alive, but he couldn't ask. Later when I think of this story, of course, I know that this was less than twenty years after the war – and the story my father's shipmate was trying to tell was most likely not one of reunion but of permanent, awful separation.

It was like a bridge between two worlds, this voyage, my father says. You know how we walk across the bridge into the city, he says, and there is that time when you are up on the walkway, high over the river, and you are not in one place and not in the other, just on the bridge, the place between? It was like that. What was behind was behind but he didn't know what was ahead. He used to go sometimes in the evenings to a room where there was a vast jigsaw puzzle – I think it had five thousand pieces! my father says – with a table all to itself. It was an Alpine scene: complicated mountains, pale blue sky, lots of grass and a few cows, not an easy puzzle and not a very exciting one either. But he would get a glass of brandy – his daily extravagance – and for a little while shift the pieces about, trying to see if this shade of cerulean blue was the same as that shade, whether male and female (he tells me that's what you call it when one piece can be inserted into another piece; I like the matter-of-factness of this) would lock together. He would not have done a jigsaw puzzle on land. I never used to think of anything while I was doing it, he says. It was very calming. I mean, just the puzzle. But I wasn't really thinking of it; just feeling my way around, and I could hear the ship's engines and maybe feel it moving, that sense of moving forward but you didn't know into what.

He's talking to himself, not to me. I don't mind. I like to listen. I don't really want to go to sleep, I wouldn't mind if he talked all night. A fire engine goes by outside. It's not an ambulance, or a police car. They make different sounds. My dad teaches me to notice the difference in things.

Time to go to sleep, he says. Enough of the ship. More tomorrow night. Okay, I say. I close my eyes, but I don't sleep. I imagine myself in the windowless cabin, the bed narrower even than mine, steel walls, the water outside, the ocean, moving forward, but you don't know into what.

* * *

Noises in the scullery. She had not seen a refrigerator; there didn't seem to be any electricity, although there was water.

He returned with a wooden board that he set on the table; there was a shoulder of brown bread on it, and a piece of yellow cheese. A knife in his hand, a big open jack-knife, hinged like a jaw. It had a black-dappled six-inch carbon blade and a wooden handle with a topaz sheen; a metal collar held the blade in place. He cut four slices from the bread and left her there; she heard a can opener, the rattle of a pan, and the click and hiss of the little stove she'd seen attached to a canister of gas.

She was very hungry. The sight of the yellow cheese and the bread made her saliva run; suddenly the drink of whisky she'd poured into her stomach turned into a knot. She didn't wait, there were no plates, but she cut a slab of the cheese with her good hand; it crumbled into curds, sharp and rank when she dropped them on her tongue. Her left hand she kept on her lap, palm up.

She heard a spoon against the sides of a saucepan. She wondered, if anyone had walked in, what they would make of the scene. Something perfectly ordinary: a man and a woman in companionable silence while one of them prepared a meal and the other sat by the fire. That was precisely how it was with her seizures, she thought: it looked ordinary, but was not. What are they like? people asked her sometimes. It was very difficult to describe. Once, she tried this: imagine you come into a room. It looks like a pleasant room. The furniture's nice and it's clean and orderly. It seems comfortable and even homely. Now, go out of the room again. The person – your friend, or a stranger – who's led you into the room now reveals what had been kept hidden before: not long ago, there was a murder in that room. All the evidence has gone, of course, but the echo of the act remains. That kind of stain can never be truly erased. Go back into the room. What do you think of it now? It is not

83

so comfortable, not so homely. You want to leave and you turn to go but you find that your friend – or the stranger – has locked the door from the outside. There is no escape. You are imprisoned with the echo of disaster; you can only wait it out. Perhaps the door will be unlocked, perhaps it will not. There is no way to know.

Still, it wasn't right, this description. People tried to envision it – police line, do not cross – but mostly, she thought, they could not. Is it like a dream? they asked. No, not like dreaming. Not like dreaming at all. And neither was this: the bread and the cheese so actual, the burn of the whisky. She would like a glass of water. She remembered the glass of water Stephen had given her at the wedding: did she wish it was Stephen who would hand her a glass of water now? What if it were Stephen who came out of the kitchen with the saucepan of soup?

She shouldn't have drunk any of the whisky, to be thinking those things. She could call Stephen. She could say: Come and get me, something terrible has happened. I'm stuck. I'm stuck with a – a madman? Stephen would laugh. Not at her, but he would not believe his capable Janet would be stuck with a madman. She didn't want to hear that laughter; did not want even to imagine it. She should want to hear it, its reassurance, its sound the sound of her own life. Her phone was in her bag, in the boot of her car. Then she doubted there would be a signal here, anyway.

She did not wish for rescue. She wished for answers, and those she would have to find herself. If this man had a key, he might have those answers, or some of them, and maybe he was not a madman anyway. Why shouldn't he think this was his house? She had not known it existed – had not known this story existed, a woman alive where a woman was dead. A woman walking in the world as she walked in the world now, who perhaps stood at the edge of the water as she had stood at the edge of the water, who had put her hand flat on the green paint of the door as she had put her hand there, had seen all this, drunk from this glass, sat by this fire. Or had not, and this was a madman, a thief, the Devil with gentle hands.

Her glass was empty. She had drunk all the whisky. He came out with two bowls of tomato soup, very plain, from a tin, and two spoons. He set them down. She would ask him.

'Can I have a glass of water?'

'Of course.'

He had sat, but rose again. The running tap. He brought it in a big white china mug and she drank. 'Thank you,' she said.

He nodded, sat again and began to spoon up the soup. He blew on it, sipped. She would say he looked almost feminine, only that wasn't quite right; yet there was something delicate about his mouth. The planes of his face were broad, though, almost coarse. His eyebrows were as pale as his hair and so almost invisible. She wished to think he was an ugly man, but could not quite bring herself to form this thought. She supposed he was about her age.

'You're not curious?' she said at last.

'About what?' Eating steadily and tidily.

'My key.'

'It's a simple key. Easily made, easily copied.'

'Why would I have copied it? How would I have got hold of yours? Why do you think yours is the original?'

'Three answers,' he smiled with his mouth closed. 'I don't know; I couldn't precisely say; and you don't know that I do.'

'This is my house,' she said.

They had finished their soup. The chipped bowls rimmed with pink scum. He cut two more pieces of bread and then pushed the blade through the rest of the cheese. He divided the food up between them.

'"My house",' he said. 'Who's "me"? Who are you?'

Why did she need to explain herself to him? Because he was here. Because there was nothing else to do.

'Janet,' she said. 'My name is Janet. Who are you?'

'I'm Tom,' he said. So they exchanged their names, very common and plain. First names, which could have been inventions. Yet the words passed between them and for an instant made a drawn thread, something tight. It was hard to tell the colour of his deep-set eyes in this light: they might have been black or green or blue. Her left hand stiffening now, inert, like a tool she had no idea how to use. She was suddenly very tired, her back aching from the drive. At the thought of going anywhere else she shivered, with exhaustion, with uncertainty, with too much knowledge and too little held together in herself, battling. Now the bread and cheese tasted of nothing, and her mouth was very dry, but she made herself eat it, and drink the water in the mug. She looked away from his steady gaze, at the table, the food, his own hand and wrist, no watch, no rings, resting broad and blunt by the knife and the heel of the bread. It was plain what she had to do, if she could drag herself to do it.

'I will call the police,' she said. 'I told you. This is my house. I inherited it. It was my mother's and now it's mine. I have papers. This is the truth. I don't know who you are, but it will be easier for you if you leave now.' Saying this, sitting there, damaged and barely able to move, but the words came as if she were still in her city office, or her home, her own place. Yet she could feel this was not her place. Her claim was flimsy and useless.

'Your mother's house?' The tilt of his head against his otherwise perfect stillness. 'Then why are you only here now? Your mother died so long ago.'

* * *

More tomorrow night, my father says, the story of the ship. But I can't sleep. I am eight, or eleven, or fifteen, or twelve, always in the same bed, my bedroom, my home. This most familiar place, the place where I started and where I think I will always be, with him, with my father. The venetian blinds never quite closed, I don't like them closed, I like the night-time light from the city to slip between the slats and keep me safe from my dreams. After the seizures this is even more important; sometimes they come before morning. They don't wake me, at least, that's not how it seems: I am allowed to waken and then they begin, pressing in on me, spinning me away from myself, dividing me, becoming me. When I have a seizure, where am I? This question occurs to me quite soon after they begin. Do I become the seizure? I feel that I do, that I am vaporized metal, electricity, air, that I could be a bright hot gas flame with all of my senses burnt away by fear, burnt away by myself.

The ones that come at night make me cry: I don't sob, I am not unhappy, but my streaming tears wet my cheeks, the pillow, the white sheets old and soft with washing and washing and washing. Until I am thirteen or fourteen – I am not sure – and decide I am too old to do this, when the night seizures come I will get up, walk down the wooden hall to my father's room and get into bed beside him. Usually he will not wake. He always sleeps on the same side of the bed, of course, most people do, by the window, his round bedside table, its books, his narrow reading glasses, the plain solid chain for his keys, his worn black billfold, a glass of water, all the things that are perfectly ordinary and could be anyone's except they are not, they are his and they are him. I crawl under the covers. Was this my mother's side? I never ask. Or if he moved to her side when she'd gone. The list of questions I have never put into words. In his bed until I know I am too old, and I don't any more, and work it out alone, the metal vapour and the tears.

Afterwards I lie still and make lists of things I've done and seen, things I want to remember. I don't keep a diary. Ruth doesn't keep a diary either. We have decided we don't like diaries, with their flimsy fake locks anyone could pull apart; who cares about hiding the key, their padded covers, their orderly lines and dates? Dear Diary. We wouldn't believe ourselves, if we read again what we wrote down. The stories change in memory and breath. It's what keeps them alive.

Stories I could make from fragments. There is no evidence; I know about destruction. This mild man, my father, who is gentle in every particular, who never raises his voice, whose assurance runs through my life with the fluidity and steadiness of an ocean current. He makes an omelette for supper: with a sharp crack he breaks the egg on the side of the bowl, with small swift flicks of his wrist he whisks the yellow and white together. The butter sizzles, welcoming, and at just the right moment he slides in the liquid, tilting the pan this way, that way, talking the while, buttering toast, tossing the salad. I sit at the kitchen table, maybe drawing, maybe telling him what I need for the next school trip; and maybe he is making spaghetti or stew. Each evening is particular, but each is the same, too, the ebb and flow of days and nights and days. We orbit each other, a planet and its moon, twin stars. Bodies drawn by the gravity of love.

He is an artist, my father. He makes technical drawings and models for architects. He makes me a dollhouse out of stiff paperboard and paints two walls as stone, two walls as clapboard wood, just as I've asked. I don't like dolls; in the house live tiny, stiff-armed bears with soldierly shoulder joints. They don't have names, the bears. There are four of them: a mother, a father and two children of indeterminate sex. I do not endow them with any interior life. They are there to sit on the perfect furniture my father makes.

He makes everything from materials he keeps in a big closet just off our apartment's front hall. It is like a cave, this closet, a treasure chest. He seems to be able to magic anything out of it. How many times have I asked, *Dad, do you have –?* And he will say, *Let's see*, and find whatever it is or something better. A particular kind of glue, a globe, some old sheet music. He has never told me that the closet – which is a mess, really, stacked with sets of wooden shelves and metal drawers, cluttered with near antique machinery (an ancient manual typewriter, a device for rolling cigarettes, even a bombsight from the Second World War) – is off limits. He has said things like, *Wait, I'll find that for you*; but I can't ever remember his forbidding me anything.

So there is no sense of transgression – I will never be able to recall such a sense – when, one afternoon, for something to do when he is out I poke idly through one stack of rattly file drawers. What do I think I might find? I am eleven. Something worth having. A pair of dice, perhaps, a pack of cards, some button or medal or tool I will be able to ask

89

about when he comes home. I had never intended to keep what I was doing secret from him.

Until I find those photographs. Colour photographs, ordinary prints, a little faded but not much. They have been torn, not in half, necessarily, but always at the edge of a figure, seated or standing. It's the first thing I notice, this tearing, because I have never seen my father tear anything. He cuts, and rarely, even, with scissors: at his elbow is always an X-acto knife and a straightedge; he will open envelopes that way or cut stars for birthday party invitations. He won't even tear open a packet of rice, but insert the tip of a knife carefully into the perforations on the box.

I run my finger along the edge of the tear. It is soft against the ball of my flesh, yet also rough; my finger can imagine the smooth edge of a photograph untorn, not mutilated. I can feel what lies behind the softness, I can feel – as in a dream that just vanishes on waking, drawing itself out of reach – violence. There are seven photographs. I wonder how long it took: all at once, quick, in a row? Or action followed by regret, by a decision to mend one's ways? I know that feeling. I remember stealing a china doll once, from my friend Molly's windowsill; a little dog slipped into my pocket. It just happened. I would put it back. I didn't. The next week, I took another. The memory of their eventual return (no hard feelings; we were still friends; these things happen) still makes my face hot. Was it like this, the tearing? I will never know. I will never ask. I hide this memory with the others, the list I keep, invisible, safe.

A rat we saw underground, waiting for a train. Looking down, my father said: See that? The dead man's switch.

Squatting by the trunk of an oak, on a day in the country, an hour away from the city. The air shimmering silver, the firestorm of the turning leaves; a little fungus that blows a puff of dun smoke, its spores. Tap it. Just like that. Hiding in the ground litter, waiting to make itself again.

One day, a chalk circle in the park, two trees, a man in black on a unicycle; his stately, ridiculous grace.

CHAPTER SIX

She sat very still. Janet. She stared at him, and he let himself be stared at. He could see she believed nothing, not even his name. What she looked for was belief. It was why she was here. Did it have his face? Her dark eyes in shadow, her left hand with its white gauze and tape nearly as bright as a lamp in the darkness. He rose and lit another lamp, and went back to the fire, adding wood and then coal too, turning his back to her again. Her telephone, her car, the threat of the police. Of course, the story could go that way. That was the way it was headed, a predictable story full of dry and meaningless words, the words of courts and hospitals.

He kept himself towards the fire, pushing at the flame with iron tongs.

'You saw that pair of seals,' he said.

'What?'

'That pair of seals,' he repeated. 'You saw them, just off shore.'

'Yes,' she said. 'I did.' Her eyes on him. One hand cradled in the other.

'I always think – they look almost human. Don't you? Have you seen them before, seals, up close like that?'

'In zoos. Never in the sea.' Her expression flat as wax. He had given her something, perhaps truth or perhaps a lie, or perhaps nothing at all. He could hold her here, if he worked at it.

'You hear stories,' he said. 'That some of them – that they're human. That they can become human. That pair,' he said to her, 'I see them a lot. I think they're male and female. I wonder who they really are. Or what.'

It was like watching someone stand on a threshold, deciding whether to cross over or turn back. He was perfectly well aware that everything she knew would be telling her to get up and leave, that truly (her clean coat, her good car, her little-used sturdy boots) whatever her life was made from, it did not need to be made from him or from this place, that as far as the turning world was concerned, she would do better to rise, to walk away and keep on walking. But he knew two things: the first, that she had come this far, this woman and her key. He knew that, and that with her arrival he seemed to have stepped back from the cliff of his own waiting. Maybe he was no longer holding his breath.

She was drawn tight like a rope, twisted on itself to fraying. 'You should sleep,' he said to her.

She laughed then, the sound was like a light. 'You're crazy,' she said. 'This is crazy. What am I doing with you? Seals? I should sleep? What the hell was that you said about my mother?'

'Did I say something about your mother?' Pulling tighter, tighter still.

'Fuck you,' she said.

*　*　*

She calls it the milk train. At first, when she says it, he thinks it will be painted white, the creamy ghost of a train travelling through the night. When they arrive at the station

93

– in a taxi – he expresses dismay. Change and disruption are countered with his own stories, too, even if those stories must be altered and altered again, like his own clothes are as he grows.

It carries the milk, she says, laughing. There is hardly anyone at the station. One man sweeps the wide plain of the station floor with a long, narrow broom; his hair is the colour of steel wire, there is a gap between his teeth through which he whistles, a tune to follow the rhythm of his sweeping, or the sweeping to follow the rhythm of his tune. Tom can't tell.

Standing, looking up to see which platform. Palm to palm. Why that moment above so many others? The touch of their hands, the broom, his fear that the sweeping man would come too close, come too close, come too close, the broom a ticking clock. There's our train, she says at last. The wind, which even at night, even in the city, is just beginning to be chased by autumn, pushes at their backs as they hurry along the grey platform. He is afraid but her step is light, she is smiling, they are leaving. He knows she likes that, always.

The carriage is empty. The light is too bright, it vibrates in his head and makes him squint. Despite himself, his body remembers being in bed and wishes to be there again. Which bed, where? He leans against her. Her arm around his shoulder, the feel of that coat, the pull of the train as it draws away, her chin on the top of his head.

He asks for riddles. Riddles cheer him up.

She sings very softly, the tune suspended in her liquid breath. Her dark head bends close to his, his own head rests against the toughened glass of the train, as they speed away, it is never flight, it is always the beginning of something, a journey towards. This is what she tells him, and he always believes her.

94

I came a-walking by your door
says the false knight on the road
it lay in your way
says the wee boy and still he stood
I flung your dog a stone
says the false knight on the road
I wish it was a bone
says the wee boy and still he stood –

Not riddles, quite, but questions and answers, which are just as good. He has always wondered what the false knight looks like. He asked her, once – she'd always sung him this song, always, as far back as his mind goes, so the tune runs through him like a vein – and she'd answered him with a question, What do you think? So he had decided that the false knight, the stranger, must look like himself, because they looked so different, she with her dark dark hair, he with his white crown. Yet the boy too would also look like him, because of course he was the boy, the boy in the song, the boy in the story, every boy, every jack. He has an image of himself, looking at himself. What would it be like to look in a mirror if you had never seen a mirror before?

I wish you were in yonder tree
says the false knight on the road
a ladder under me
says the wee boy and still he stood
the ladder it will break
said the false knight on the road
and you will surely fall
says the wee boy and still he stood –

Now perhaps the boy is sorry he asked for riddles, sorry she is singing this song, because it makes him wonder. He knows she does not like it when he wonders, this particular question that troubles him but does not trouble her, what made him. When he was smaller and didn't understand how these things worked (he still does not understand, not exactly, but better than he used to), he'd ask her, How did you choose me? Because she would sometimes say, *You are my favourite boy* – and so he knew that must mean that there had been other boys, that there must have been a choice. He'd imagined her holding out her long white arm as she pointed and said, Yes, that one. He's the boy for me. *My boy*. My choice. *I just did,* she would answer. *I chose you.*

All by herself, she would have chosen, because that's how she always did things. Well, all by herself, and with him. Yet now – their bodies pressed close on the train, he's not cold, but he's tired, and sometimes it feels the same – he knows that they are not alike, that they are less and less alike, they are certainly not the same person, which is sometimes what he used to think. Who falls when the ladder breaks? This is different from rock-a-bye baby, that doesn't scare him, that's never scared him, a nursery rhyme, but now when he thinks of the man, the boy, the tree, the ladder, he worries he is not as clever as the boy in the story and that it might be him who would fall. How does the boy know that the knight is false? What does *false* mean? Pretending to be something he's not, he guesses. But how does that seem to the boy, when he and the man are wearing the same face?

* * *

Once she had eaten, Janet looked steadier, ruddier. The firelight, the oil light, made her look younger than she must be. How old? She is, he thought, like him, in the middle: past the beginning, still far from the end. Looking for a clearing, or a way to choose a path.

Silence, after she swore at him. He didn't flinch, because he has learnt to tell a feint from a blow.

She rose up then, stood. First her injured hand dropped down by her side; but she must have felt the thud of the blood in the still-open wound because she quickly raised it, crossed it over her chest and held it there. Moved away from the fire and walked towards the front door, which she opened, letting the wind in, but she stood on the sill without her coat, the flames behind her bowing away from the gusts and then lifting their heads again as if they were as curious as he. Her hair pushed back from her face, slipping out of its plait; he thought there were silver threads in it, but it was hard to tell. She stood on the balls of her feet. Her desire to run held in check, reined in hard until its mouth was bloody as her palm.

'I'm going to phone,' she said. Then she walked out of the door and did not close it behind her. The wind made it bang. He sat. Her tread on the gravel, in the dark that must have clustered around her. Night came quickly here, the lid of a closing eye. Sounds of no importance: the neutral, nearly cheerful bleat of her car as she opened it with an infrared beam. One door, the boot, no sound from her voice, not that he could hear anyway, and then she was walking back, her footsteps heavier on the gravel, a little slower. She was carrying something.

Her eyes were wide when she came back in the house, as if she'd tried to devour the darkness with her gaze. She had two bags: a small black nylon rucksack and a leather case, shaped like an old carpetbag, not much bigger. Both of them over her right shoulder so she was unbalanced; she dropped them with a thud to the flagged floor. The door shut. He didn't move, sat very still, watched her as she dug in the black bag for her phone. She peered at it; wandered around the small room, staring at its screen.

'Reception's not very good here, I'm told,' he said.

'No,' she said. 'It's not. There was nothing by the car.' Now she stood by the fire. She pressed a button, just one, and held the little machine close to her ear. She saw him watching her. She would rather have been outside, he could see that. He could have stood, walked outside himself. He did not. He did look away, at the hearth, the quick illusion of privacy leaping up between them like a flame.

'I'm here,' she said. 'Can you hear me?'

One half of the conversation.

'I know. I know, not very good.'

Her voice banging against the stone walls of the place, too loud.

'Long. But it was okay.'

The drive, she must mean.

'Well, it's hard to say. Yes, yes, the key was fine.'

An elision. The first. There would be more.

'It's all fine. It's – strange. Hard to describe on the phone. I'll tell you – are you there?'

She was looking down hard at the stone floor, as if there would be a face in that rippled surface, a solid mirror of distance; then back at the little screen of the phone, then pushing it against her ear again.

'I'm fine.' She was nearly shouting. 'Don't worry. Listen, tomorrow I'll go somewhere where we can hear better. I'll ring you tomorrow. Okay? Okay? Can you –?'

She had turned away from him, only just, not completely, curling the phone against her ear as if to soothe it. He noticed that she had not lied. There were no lies, here, just now, in this room.

Silence enough for a breath.

'Me too. Me too.' She nodded. She did not say goodbye. Another button pressed, and one more. Her shoulders dropped after the effort of making herself heard, after the effort, he thought, of parrying whatever questions she could hardly hear. She returned to the table, sat, set the phone down, reached for the knife and cut herself another hunk of cheese and began to eat, looking at nothing, the wooden surface, the floor, the stone wall, her eyes flickering everywhere and nowhere. Her bandaged hand. She held herself very straight, containing everything.

'You didn't call the police, then,' he said at last.

'Apparently not.'

'So who was that?'

'None of your goddamn business.'

He shrugged. He too ate a piece of cheese. He reached for the bottle of whisky, lifted it and held it up to her; she did not refuse.

'He won't come looking for you?'

She laughed, or seemed to.

'No,' she said. 'He won't.'

'You could be anywhere. With anyone.'

'No,' she said, 'I couldn't. I'm here. With no one. That's what I said.'

'It isn't,' he answered. 'That's not what I heard. You said you were here. You didn't say you were alone.'

Did she colour? Impossible to tell. Too dark. Her face still flushed by the fire.

'I didn't say anything.'

'Why not?' One step again over the threshold. It was like imagining his own hands flat against her chest, pushing.

She looked amused now. 'You have no right to ask that. Absolutely no right. To ask anything. Anything of me.'

'"No right"?' he said. 'I don't know what you mean.'

'I can see that,' she said, and with her good hand gestured around her, at what he had taken possession of.

He saw then how well he had shuttered himself away, that she saw nothing of him. That she had expected one thing and found another, and since then he had boxed her in, hardly allowing her sight or breath. What he had given her – the food, the binding of her wound – had seemed an intrusion or imposition. Nothing he had said or done was a trick, but she had felt tricked all the same. She was at a limit now, a wall: she had made a choice, but it was not too late to turn back, to change her mind, to travel the obvious path.

All he knew was that he did not want her to leave; and only now did he see that she might, of course she might, she should – she was afraid and he was the one who had made her so. In her eyes he could only see a flatness, a deadness, that would not recognise the connection he knew existed between them. He'd seen it, that connection, as soon as he'd seen her face, felt its familiarity in his heart, remembered an embrace. That long-gone embrace, that long-gone voice, the stories he'd heard as a child – not from this mouth, but a mouth so like it. Standing before her, knowing suddenly and completely that in the next moment he might be lost, be left again, he felt – something that was not familiar. That might be loneliness. That might be fear. What he had worked so hard to keep at a distance from himself, to ignore and to bury. But that he should be abandoned by this woman, that he could not bear.

It was so clear in her face what she thought. He had told her he was not a thief; why should she believe that? He could be nothing else to her. Loathing himself suddenly for making her think that, for his desire to frighten her. He had desired that. Had he been frightened himself? That hunter who'd stood on the shore, waiting for the woman, the seal, to rise out of the sea in her shining skin: he had never thought that the hunter might have been afraid. His heart in his chest was heavy and bright as gold.

'Please,' his mouth made the word. 'This is not what you think.'

Her narrowed eyes. 'What isn't? You? Who the hell cares about you?'

'Please.' He exhaled; let something out of him. Let her in. Let her in. She sensed the change. He could see it in the tilt of her head, the rhythm of her own breathing. She was listening to something now. It was not only his words.

'What you said before,' she said. 'About my mother. Where did that come from? What do you know?' The strain in her face, one hand gripped into a fist, squeezing the empty air, her own skin and bone.

'Nothing,' he said. 'Not yet. Or only one thing. That I've been waiting for something. You.'

* * *

Blackberries on the lane where they walk. The path dips and curves and the hedges, thick with late-summer fruit, rise high on either side of them. It's good to be out of the city, however much he had not wanted to leave. This is how it always is: now that they are here (wherever here is), it is all right, because she makes it so. The places change and change again, and all the other faces change, but hers does not, not her face and not her voice. He had thought they were in a hurry as they walked along – he didn't know where they were going, he hardly ever asked – but now they dawdle, she allows it, and she pulls from her pocket a little bag, plain brown paper, catches it open and hands it to him so he can gather the berries. He gathers and eats, eats and gathers, the air smells of salt and the sea and makes the berries taste sweeter than they truly are.

She seems happy, she is singing, not looking at him, sometimes reaching into the brambles to pick the berries with him and drop them into his bag. Both of their hands stained with the dark juice, both of their hands pricked and scratched by the little thorns that try in vain to protect their hoard.

I wish you were in yonder sea
Says the false knight on the road –

What will they do with all this fruit? She has never made jam, or a pie, not that he can remember. Perhaps they will simply live off it, like birds. He never knows what they are going to eat from day to day; sometimes it is just things in tins, baked beans or sweet mandarins – she likes those, she always has – and sometimes she will cook. Although she says she is not very good at it, he will always exclaim over what she's made, a dry pork chop and a baked potato, broccoli and lumpy gravy. All done on two burners in a bedsit, almost a camping stove, her white brow drawn tight with the effort, though she would always laugh at herself. Sometimes, if they had money and were in a city – he never knew really how this happened, how there would suddenly be banknotes, greasy with potential, in her purse – they would go to a restaurant, just the two of them, or some-times (but rarely) with one of her friends, in which case the money wouldn't come out of her purse, though he would know it was there. Once (he had been wearing a tie, he had been sitting up very straight) they had caviar. He hadn't believed it was eggs. He must have been about seven. It was oily and dense, like a fishy thundercloud, the silvery colour of seacoal, and it came with a tiny spoon made of pearl which he stole. He remembered that meal not because of the caviar, really, which he had liked well enough, but because he had still been hungry afterwards.

So perhaps it would be blackberries now, blackberries to the end of the week, or the month; perhaps that's all there was, in this new place. Yet she didn't seem worried, the way she sometimes did when they arrived somewhere.

A good boat under me
says the wee boy and still he stood –

It had been a fine morning, washed blue; but now ragged white balls of cloud with shadows at their centres had come scudding over the inland hills and running up from the horizon. When they hid the sun his blue windcheater was suddenly not warm enough, and the little hairs at the back of his neck would rise. She was wearing her old sweater, one she said had been her father's, thick, black, indestructible and always smelling of smoke no matter how much she washed it. They had stayed in a hotel last night, a big white house a few miles from here, close to the beach. Funny how crowded it had seemed, though there were few people there, but it was a warren of small rooms and long corridors, the carpet everywhere in dark colours, blood and wood and leaf green, thick swirls of colour that ran under his feet like a heaving sea. They'd stayed in hotels before, though not often, and he wasn't sure he liked this place, the sense he had of being watched. There was a young woman in a stiff white apron who looked as if she disapproved of something, maybe everything. She'd led them to the room (at the back, over the car park, not over the sea, and until late he'd lain and heard cars revving, coughing, moving away and toward) with its one bed, small window, a sink in the corner with a cracked pink cake of soap in a tray. But he'd liked the dinner they'd had in the restaurant, roast beef and Yorkshire pudding and carrots cooked until they were soft and sweet. The gravy was brown and salty, and when he was done he dipped his bread roll into it to catch it all. She had watched him, smiling. She had had a big plate of food like his, but she didn't eat much; that was normal.

She was always in movement. At school (any one of the schools he'd been to), if it was him, they would have called it fidgeting, and told him to stop. He was not a fidgeter, but she was, pushing the food around her plate with her fork, a bite here and a bite there, not much, shifting in her seat, smiling too broadly at that girl, the girl in the stiff apron, now serving them too, bringing milk for him and a glass of wine, red wine, for her. She'd raised it to him, when it came, her glass, and he knew to lift his too.

To us, she'd said, and sipped the wine, and he'd drunk his milk and eaten his dinner and watched as she watched the room and while he ate a bowl of chocolate ice cream she pulled a pack of cigarettes from her bag and shook it: the last one. Digging for matches in the bottom of her bag; she had to try three, scratch, scratch, before one would light. She closed her eyes to pull the smoke into her lungs. He didn't like her cigarettes, the smell of them, except in that first instant of lighting; the paper, the tobacco, the match in that moment made a quick scent that to him was somehow home, though he couldn't have explained that. The sound of it, the fire, her breath, inhaling and exhaling.

In the morning, packing their small bag. Her underwear, her tights, drying on the radiator of the room, the smell of soap and damp last night. She had squeezed them in the little corner sink, her knuckles red. Handing over money to the woman behind the reception desk; the woman's incurious gaze. With strangers he liked to believe he was invisible. As she counted the bills, he practised standing as still as he could, like a game of statues that would not end, sinking his heels into the thick carpet, the soles of his feet there, his hands down by his sides, his breath shallow in his nose. The woman gone, the smell of bacon, the window, the pen, the money. Himself. All gone.

And now in this lane, seeking whatever was at the end of it. She was moving so slowly, but why there was no way of knowing. They had thumbed a lift to get here – it was something she did a lot. This time in a little white pickup truck, smelling of farms, sharp, sweet, slightly rotten. The driver was a young man in a thick dirty white sweater, the grime under his nails, the brown plastic steering wheel, the three of them in the single front seat, a clutter of nylon rope and implements under her feet, the man's hand on the gear-stick on the switchback road. He hardly spoke to them – they were not in the cab for more than ten minutes – just nodded, said: Where to? and she had said, Thank you, and the name of the next town – only, not so far, she said, I'll tell you where. When she'd indicated the green verge where he'd left them, the young man had said, Are you sure? but nothing more. She had thanked him again, and so had he, because he knew already to be polite to the strangers whose small, intangible gifts sometimes meant the fulfilment of her desires. The truck driving away, a grey canvas tarpaulin stretched over its back, the sound of its engine dying into the sound of the sea. Years later, wondering if she ever imagined the danger of these encounters, that anything might happen to her in a stranger's car, to her or to him. His dreams of being stolen. His dreams that she vanished. The red taillights of a strange car, driving away, driving away: who was in the car he never knew.

His brown paper bag is heavier now, it is nearly full. There is a stain at the bottom, spreading blots where the berries have begun to crush themselves with their own weight and bleed their juice. The lane is sloping down towards where he sees it bend away around the hedge, and she is just ahead of him, with more purpose in her step now, seeming to allow him to dawdle, fruitpicking, if he wants, though it's hard to tell which of them keeps the other back.

The boat will surely sink
says the false knight on the road –

Who will wait round the bend? He has decided it will be someone, not something, or has she decided this? What does she know? He knows nothing. He knows from her footsteps, somehow, that she has been here before, that she is not following directions but memory, something imprinted in her as she is herself imprinted into him.

Then, before they round the corner, she turns to him. She is facing him. Her back is to the sea, which is greyer now than it was before. The clouds pile up on themselves, darker at their edges, a rim of threat. She kneels down, her skirt over her thighs, she spreads it flat with her fine-boned hands in a gesture he knows she makes when she is nervous, and he can see the bright light in her eyes that is no reflection, that comes from inside, the lit wick that wires up from her heart. He can feel it beating when she puts her arms around him, first on his shoulders, as if she is testing what he is made from. Are they made out of the same stuff? Bones, blood, breath? She takes the twisted neck of the blackberry bag out of his hand and sets it lightly on the gravel – and then puts her arms right round him, holding

106

him tight so fast he doesn't have a chance to hug her himself, his own arms are imprisoned against his sides and his face is in her dark hair, her neck, this safe place, the sound of her breathing against the susurration of the sea, the beat of her heart against his own. She kisses his cheek, his temple, with her soft smoky mouth.

I'm so glad we came, she says. *You're with me here. I'm so glad.*

He has no idea. He is with her. That is important. He wants to hold her, but if he tries it will seem, maybe, as if he is trying to break away from her clasp.

The wind rises, just then, as if a door had been opened somewhere and let in a draught. Push and pull, first against her back, then against his, and he will always remember this instant, this instant before, the wall of the hedge, the clouds, the salt smell, the bumpy gravel under his sneakers, his warmth in her embrace.

Come on, she says, *let's go.*

She is moving quickly now, striding, he nearly forgets to bend, to collect his precious bag of sour-sweet fruit, one hand for the bag and one hand for her, and there it is, around the bend, of course he knew it would be there, the little house, its peeling green door, its eyeless stare, its attention, a place folded in on itself, built of stone, of the future, of the past.

The door opens. It swings of its own accord. He squeezes her hand, he could not call this terror, he does not know if it has a name, some wild delight, some vertigo. The dark mouth of the door –

And you will surely drown
Says the wee boy and still he stood –

CHAPTER SEVEN

Waiting for you. His deep-set eyes were in shadow, unreadable. He had not moved from the table; the bottle of whisky was by his elbow, the cheese, the bread, their shapes, tastes and textures recognisable and yet no longer reassuring. That at least was familiar, like the taste of metal in her mouth, the other world she knew. Maybe she could be at home here. The door had banged behind her and she had felt the wind on her back. It had been possible to imagine, though she could not have said why, that as that door shut another door opened. This small stone room bigger than it seemed, containing another universe, containing him.

Stephen's voice, so calm. She thought of the astronauts, the weak beam fired through space, the last contact, and then the dark side of the moon. It was a choice to go there, to travel in this way.

Waiting for you. She looked hard at him. His voice was deep, and somehow – plain. It made a clear sound in her head, like a bell.

Her phone, small and light with its green, glittering single eye, was still in her hand. She bent down and set it carefully on the stone floor, and then she lifted her foot and put her heel against it. Her weight transferred: one clean crack and then the thing came apart under her sole.

Even in the half-light she could see his eyes widen, the tilt of his head, his open mouth. And then he laughed, his head right back, the jut of his Adam's apple, the hollow at the base of his throat. He took the last dregs of the whisky into his mouth and set the glass down on the table. Sitting staring at her, and she was standing still there, the link severed. Swung around by gravity into darkness and silence, into the absolute.

He got up. He didn't take his eyes off her. His gaze, collecting her. He got the dustpan and brush again, with a shrug, as if it were funny, and it was, she was grinning, exhausted suddenly, her body soft but still upright, and he came towards her, kneeling down to sweep the crumbs of plastic away, to chase them over the stone, chips of it and metal and wire, glittering a little in the firelight. *Hush, hush*, went the brush over the stone, it was like the sound of the sea, and then he touched her calf to make her raise her leg so he could sweep beneath her foot. Standing on one leg. Her bad hand clutched to her chest still, throbbing, though the pain was almost pleasant now, a reminder she was alive.

The patter of the waste into the bin, softer than the sound of the glass had been, although she thought it should have been louder, loud as an alarm. She did not feel afraid.

How many words had she heard over the years? She wondered if it was possible to count. Every *a*, every *of*, every *this*. Pouring through her head, a river of language, listening, she was always listening, always attentive, always waiting for the single word, the chain of words, that would change things, solve the problem. What was the problem? She wouldn't know until she heard the words. There was no such thing as the same old story. You went to meet the story and the story came to you. Stephen, Stephen.

Stephen's stories were told without words, she hardly understood them although they spoke to her all the same, she knew they did, and there had been nights when she would lie stretched naked on the bed and he would stand over her, his long body swaying like a tree in the wind, the violin under his chin and his eyes closed, playing for her. It was funny, of course it was funny, they laughed, the naked violinist! But it was more than funny too. It was real, this voice of his, complex, comprehensible, hidden. Stephen. His voice, the voice of his mouth in her ear. Everything's all right? I'm fine. *I'm fine.*

She had been fine since she was three years old. Of course I'm fine. Your mother died so long ago.

She had closed her eyes. She opened them and there he was in the firelight. Not so much taller than she was. The thick wild hair, nearly white, such a strange colour to find on a grown man.

Stephen's gentle voice, persuasive. Wait for me. I'll come with you. How she hated him then. It should have been strange to her, the violence of that emotion, but it had been the only word she could find. She was gone already. It was no good.

She had never been in such a place as this. Now she recalled the drive as something that had sucked her forward into a vortex, a maelstrom, a place on the other side. The calm and silence of the vacuum. There was nothing to be afraid of. She was shaking. She was afraid.

He was watching her. Suddenly she wondered if she had been speaking, all her thoughts let out in the air without her knowledge. His blueblack stare as if he heard something she could not. It would have been possible to believe it was her own voice. Why? In this place, this stone place, the sea outside, dropped off the edge of the world. The void. His hand on her calf, the certainty of that. He was just standing there. He did not move.

* * *

It was so cold that winter, my father says. He is sitting on the edge of my bed. It's too late. I can't sleep. I call him and he comes. His hand in my hair, pulling the comforter over me, holding my hand.

I know it gets cold here, he says. Probably colder. I'm sure it's colder. But the thing was – that winter, there – well, you couldn't get warm. Most of the time you couldn't get warm, anyway, even before that winter came. It's hard to say why. (When he talks like this, it's almost like he's talking to himself. I don't mind. I like it. It means he'll go on, he'll forget how late it is. He himself becomes the story, I decide.) You'd stand right by the fire in someone's house and sure enough, your front would be warm, your face would be boiling, but the back of you . . .

It could be the summer, that he's telling me this story, a summer night and the city's wet breath is pressing against the glass. The air-conditioning straining against it like sailors manning the pumps against a flood, the ratcheting whirr and hum. Sirens, there are always more sirens in the summer, more fires, more fights, more disturbances making blazes of every description. The river oily outside in the darkness, pouring back the day's heat into the air. Almost impossible – yet so pleasurable – to imagine the freezing cold, the cold when you can't get warm, just as he says. What's that like? I think of stripping off snowboots, skipants, parka, quick as I can, my cheeks already stained from the warmth off the big brass radiators in the school lobby. My cheeks flushing with the sudden heat as they'd flush with cold outside. The weather at bay. Warmth every-where. Warmth was the truth, the cold was a lie, or at least, something temporary.

But in the story he tells, the cold is the truth. Your face would be boiling, but the back of you – well, you'd turn and turn like a pig on a spit, just hoping to get every bit of you warm at once! But it was impossible. You'd get dizzy! And we'd both laugh.

He'd found a cheap room at one end of the city, in the west. In a coffee bar he'd seen a little index card, pinned on a board: so much rent, evening meals included. There was an electric fire in the room, he says. I'd never seen one, it seemed like a funny old thing. There was electricity; there was fire; I could see how they were related, but they were not at all the same. So he describes the three glowing bars that threw off as much orange light as they did heat (maybe more light) and they stopped doing either unless you put a coin, and another and another, into the little slot at the side. He didn't have that many coins.

I know the story so well. There are parts of it I know less well than others: the early parts, when the ship first left him at the dock and he got straight on another, a ferry that took him across that crowded channel. Then in another country where, standing by the side of the road with the sour taste of strange bread in his mouth, he stuck out his thumb for a lift. Miles of road, months of travel, so many languages, so many strangers, nearly all of them smiling. Sometimes he says: I could have told them anything. I thought that again and again. Every person I met I could have told a different story about who I was and where I was going. I could have said, I'm from Texas. Or: I'm going to be a doctor. Or: I'm only telling you this, but really, I'm a spy.

I laugh, listening to this. What else could you have said?

Anything. What do you think?

You could have said: I'm a bullfighter. I have a book about bullfights. A book about a bull who won't fight.

I saw some of those, he said. I don't think they would have believed me.

What was it like? There is a first time for every question.

The bullfight? Hot. It was like – ancient times. Like gladiators. I tried to like it, but I felt sorry for the bull. That's why I think they wouldn't have believed me.

I wonder if I would feel sorry for the bull. I would like to find out.

An astronaut?

His laugh is everything, is the whole shape of him. There were hardly any astronauts then. There aren't many now, you know that. And again, I'm not sure I would have convinced them.

So you told them the truth?

I guess I did, he says. I told them the truth.

But it is winter I like best, the story of that winter when they met. When he'd come back at last to the country where the ship had first set him ashore, this old place with its bad plumbing, gallons of milky tea and long green walls of ancient hedge. Its great city burnt and rebuilt, not once but twice. The country where he'd find her, in the end, his one true love, his wife, my mother.

So, there was my room and there was my job, he says. I didn't have any money left, so I had to get a job.

I see it all, as he tells her story: the pictures are vivid in my mind although I have never been to the places he speaks of. It doesn't matter that when I go there – much later, when I travel to the place he'd travelled to in order to make my own life for my own reasons, certainly they are my own reasons – it doesn't matter that the pictures have little bearing on reality. The two don't jar; they make a dialogue with each other, the dialogue between the story and the truth. The same and not the same. The story is always real. The story of his work, the wet cloth in his hand, one day, one winter afternoon, in the thick brown fug that drifts from the endless rolled cigarettes, hangs in the worn carpet, the shiny velvet of the barstools, the little heads of pickled eggs in a big jar, the slick damp surface of the bar.

All the conversations, heard and half-heard. How's it going, Yank? It's what they called me, he says. A lot of them didn't have teeth, you know, I noticed that, and then they would admire mine. I wore my scarf indoors. The soles of my shoes were too thin. (All this I can recall, his voice in fragments, the story threaded together like beads.)

It's the cold I want. The ice piling up on the pavement, thick. No one has the right shoes; nails and leather sliding, sliding, the palm of your naked hand on the ice to break your fall. He is hunching over, he is walking through the ice, the snow, he's wondering if the pipes have frozen (I'd pour a kettle of water down the toilet, I'd hope that would help, the pipes banging as if there were someone down there trying to get out, it would wake me in the night). He's laughing now, always laughing about this cold, but then he had chilblains, he started to feel tired all the time, the shivering wore him out, the cold boring into him like dark blue light.

I was walking home, he says. Well, I'd got the bus, I always got the bus, and I never got over climbing to the top, even after weeks had passed, even though the windows were fogged with breath and the frozen city vanished under the mist of all that life, the inhale and exhale of the effort to go on. I was walking home from the bus, it was dark, it got dark so early, the lamplight was yellow and there wasn't much of it and the place seemed so quiet, like all the city's noise had frozen too. Funny what you remember. I remember seeing that a dog, I guess, had peed, or it could have been a person, and the pee had just frozen there, this yellow streak a little sunk into the ice. Why do I remember that? Seeing that before I heard her voice.

He is talking to himself. No, I never stop him.

She was standing on the steps. Her legs were blue with the cold. I could hear her. Damn and blast. Damn it all. Fuck.

He says that word. He doesn't mean to. He realises what he's done. But he can't stop talking to himself.

Sorry, he says. But that's what she said. No one said it, in those days. They shouldn't now, of course. His half-smile. A lost smile. Smoothing the comforter again, my hair, holding my hand. The heat outside. The sirens again, wailing another sad tale.

She'd lost her key, he says.

* * *

'I am tired,' she said to him. 'Yes, I'm tired.' As if they had known each other for years and she had arrived here, the expected guest made to feel at home with whisky, canned soup and a bandage for her palm, the traditional welcome in this brand-new country. What country? Where he belonged and where she found herself. If she could describe this place and the sensation of being here, it would be as good as describing those electrical storms in her head.

It occurred to her then that she might be having a seizure. Had she ever had one and not known? Not that she was aware of: but then, of course she would not have been aware. A paradox.

Could she have said the seizures were like being pressed against glass? Yes. A glass door. Imprisoned against it, held by a force, unable to step back or forward. Closed off from everything: the trick would be to step through the glass, the terror was being alone, cut off, even from the familiar carpet beneath her heel, the dishes in the cabinets, the spoons in the sink, the familiar dragged away but left visible, tantalising, just out of reach. If she could only – if she could only – that was the feeling, the fear, that she could never, never get there, wherever there was. It was where she most wanted to go. It was where she was most afraid of. Where was it? The taste of it was always the same, the metal taste, no matter where she was, how it struck her.

The taste of this place. She could not express it. She had been pushed through the glass. Finally. She stood on the other side. This stone house, on the other side of the glass.

Or she'd had too much whisky. Give him nothing. Not even, I'm tired. Too late now.

'Then you should sleep,' he said. 'You've had a long journey. I have some painkillers, if you want. There's the sink in the kitchen if you want to wash; the toilet's round the back. Nothing very grand.'

'I didn't know if there was a toilet at all,' she said. 'Thanks.'

They smiled at the same time. His crooked face. As fair as she was dark; the pale creases at the corners of his eyes where the sunlight could not reach.

'I have a toothbrush in my bag,' she said, and did not move.

'Then you'd better get it,' he said. 'Not that I insist you brush your teeth.'

The sense of something tearing, when she rose. Not tearing. Stretching. As if he had been touching her and she had pulled away, but he had not.

116

One-handed, she dug in her bag for her wash kit. He led her back into the little bare kitchen, hardly a room at all, a cramped stone shunt off the side of the house with another door leading out the back, facing the sea. 'That way,' he said, pointing through it. 'And there's some pills above the sink.'

'Thanks,' she said.

By the light of the oil lamp she brushed her teeth. It was complicated. She wanted to keep her left hand still, but it was impossible not to use it at all. She held her tube of toothpaste down on the wooden draining rack by the big stone sink with the side of her hand, pressed and squeezed, hard enough to reawaken the cut. Her heart in her palm, beating. Hard to see in this light, but she thought it had stopped bleeding.

She looked up, out through the dirty glass of the window. The day closing its eye, night opening, spreading itself, its rich blue staining the fields, the stones, turning the water into a steely sheet, rippled as chain mail. Night drew the distance between her and her home to even greater lengths. Her home, their home, the place they'd made together, Stephen standing on a chair to change a lightbulb or at long last in the garden, hacking at the rosebush with rusty secateurs and swearing. Then she was not grateful to him, though she should have been. Then he was on tour, then she was alone, then she was glad. Then it was home, only then, when she was there by herself. There was no moment when her acceptance of his love, their life, had become a seal, a closing-off, and yet it had happened. The high price of kindness, exchanging the gift of the self. There she had been, the night before this, a hundred years ago, standing at the clean white sink in her clean bright bathroom, whole, squeezing the tube, moving around the inside of her mouth with her brush, early to bed because of the long journey in the morning, Stephen going from room to room as if he couldn't settle. He could not. She did not ask, *What's wrong?* because she knew.

Love that lengthens, thins.

How many truces until the last truce is reached? If there is truce, has there been war?

She could see her reflection in the glass. The balance of light was changing; suddenly the tilt of the earth meant that the lamp's flame lit her and gave her back to herself. There was no mirror here (she didn't think there would be one in the toilet) and it was like looking down into the water to see herself in the window, there. She leaned closer. If she were a stranger, looking at herself, what would she have read in her face?

Fear meant no forward movement. Fear was frozen. She was not frozen. She was in motion. Footsteps behind her, Tom in the stone room by the fire, in this house. Her own face told her nothing. She spat into the sink, rinsed her mouth with the water that splashed down hard from the tap, wiped with her sleeve at the window glass, but could see herself no more clearly.

The wind had risen. It batted at her when she opened the plain wooden door that led to another little door, which she opened too. The deep black, the smell of bleach. She went back for the oil lamp, leaving the latches on both doors lifted so she wouldn't have to manage the lamp and the latches with one hand.

It was cold in this small room. The toilet had an old-fashioned high tank with a chain. She set the lamp on the floor and then began to manage the business of undoing her leather belt, the buttons on her trousers, with one hand, holding the fabric against herself with her left wrist, which didn't help much. Suddenly she had to pee very badly, the soup, the whisky, the water. Her jeans were stiff, her legs were trembling, the hairs on her thighs rising against the cloth. Christ. She could manage what had happened so far; she couldn't manage explaining that she'd wet herself.

There, her jeans around her ankles: she dropped down on to the seat and leant her forehead into her hand. The floor in here was cement, rough. She lifted her head; she could reach out and touch the wood of the door. A roll of toilet paper hung neatly on it. The toilet paper appeared to be pink, which for some reason amused her. The wood was soft, splintery. This was newer than the rest of the house, at least she thought so, not that she had any experience of thinking about such things. But it can't have been too new. It must have been here, this toilet (it seemed important, it seemed practical, in stories no one had to use the toilet but real life – real life – was a trip from toilet to toilet), when her mother –

Or it wasn't here. Her mother was never here. Just because the key came from her mother it didn't mean –

The size of that particular joke was difficult to conceive of. Not my house. A house. Who cares? A collection of stones and glass, wooden planks and a half-antique john. No place was important. No place held a trace of the dead, not if you couldn't pull the thread yourself, see the connection, make the link. But if Tom –

Tommy was a piper's son
he learnt to play when he was young
but all the tune that he could play
was over the hills and far away –

She had that song on a tape when she was a girl. The words were nothing, but the tune on the tape had always haunted her, the rise and fall that held the roll of the land in its music. Tommy who was not much use but could do one thing well. A single offering. Over the hills and far away –

Pink toilet paper. She stood up, pulled the chain, hauled up her jeans but gave up on redoing the buttons, letting her sweater hang over the front. The lamp and the dark, the wind outside sluicing around the lantern's glass, the flame miraculously unperturbed, a little sucked and fluttering from the air that passed over the clear chimney, that's all. Back in the kitchen, running her hand under the cold water from the tap, the rough bar of cracked white soap.

Exhaustion overcame her and her veins filled with lead. She would think about it in the morning, all of it: she would disappear into this night. She remembered how once, when she was a girl – thirteen – she had gone to France over the summer. It had been arranged she would stay with a family outside a small northern town that had little to recommend it other than that its inhabitants spoke French, and improving her French had been the point of the journey. The family were nice enough – a mother, a father, two children, a girl a year older and a boy a year younger. She was given a bicycle. She could pedal round the narrow, bleak lanes under a plain white sky by herself; she could buy bread in the morning. Sometimes she went with the boy, who would stare at her and rarely spoke. The mother was kind; she was an ambulance driver, and this made every trip in the family car something of an adventure. But what Janet recalled now was the anxiety that never really left her. None of the food (which she was certain was good) tasted of much; there were green beans with olive oil and garlic, there was chicken cooked in wine, but she was afraid, afraid of saying the wrong thing with the wrong words. She didn't want to be here, she wanted to be home, even though she knew there was nothing to be afraid of.

The only solution she found was darkness. At home, at night, she loved the orange city light spilling through the blinds, the yellow incandescence from the bathroom, the living room, the hall. Her bedroom door wide open, Come in. In this house, in this strange country, her room had a thick wooden door and on the window there were tall wooden shutters that could be closed with an iron latch, they were like doors themselves. They were painted a dull brown and the iron was dull black. When they were closed, and when the door was closed, the room became almost completely dark. Cavernous black. No, not quite: the first night she took the towel they'd left her, rolled it into a terrycloth snake, shoved it down right at the base of the door where a space between the planks and the carpet let in a slice of hallway light. The towel was almost exactly the same width as the door, which was good. Now, black. Her hand in front of her face. Nothing. The relief of it, like being able to disappear. She could have been anywhere. The black could take her away from here, from the strangers, take her home.

Janet brought that black back to herself now as she passed from the kitchen into the single stone room of this place. The iron bed with its chipped white paint, the thin mattress, worn sheet and bedding. Not a single bed, but not a double bed either. All she wanted was to be horizontal.

The oil lamp in her hand, another on the table where Tom was sitting on one of the two chairs. She passed by him. The movement of the air between them. Whether he was watching her or not. No scent of him, in the air. Woodsmoke, water, damp, the oil in the lamps.

'I'm going to sleep,' she said. Walking to the bed, sitting on its edge. He did not move. He must be watching her. The windows sheeted with the blue spill of starlight. There was a wooden table by the bed; she set the lamp on it and sat down. She peered at the flame. 'How does it –?' she asked. She touched the glass with her good hand, then drew back from the heat.

He rose and walked towards her and knelt at her feet. Without speaking he reached out for her left foot and swiftly undid the knot in her lace, loosening, loosening down the path of her ankle, the rise of her metatarsal, working off the boot. Her mouth was open and she closed it. She could see the double crown of his pale head as he bent, and took off her other boot with the same exactness. His hand just below her calves to hold her still. Her socks were dark green wool.

He didn't seem to mind the heat of the glass. He lifted the globe, blew the flame, and now the room was nearly in darkness. The light of the fire dying, shadows giving expression to his face, expression she could not really see or could not, at least, believe, as he looked up at her and she looked down at him, two strangers at the edge of the land, two strangers in the shadows of themselves.

He did not wish her goodnight. He simply lifted himself to his feet again and in the meagre light began quietly to clear the things from the table and bring them into the kitchen. Janet swung her legs up into the bed, dug them under the covers and lay down on her back with her injured hand crossed over her chest. As soon as she closed her eyes, she slept.

* * *

In my dream she is standing now. The white gown that I have never seen before falls along the length of her body, the cloth almost sheer down from the close-worked neck.

The grass over her grave is quite smooth, her rising has not disturbed it and now I can see – because she has moved away from where she had been resting – that there is no date on the headstone, no second date, that is. There is her name, and the date of her birth, and the dash. Nothing else. There is yellow lichen spreading into the grooves of the carved letters, over the *M* and the *a* of her first name, the *t* at its end. The lichen almost glows in the queer violet light here, beacons or eyes.

I hand her the baby. I didn't know there was a baby until I held out my arms towards her and felt the weight of the little body there. The baby is wrapped tight in cloth, like a baby in an old painting. Its legs move in the binding, a maggoty wriggle. I don't know how old the baby is, except that it is tiny; had I held it against my breast, comforted it, rocked it? I don't think so. Even in the dream I think that feeling would be inside me, if I had. The baby has dark hair and dark eyes and the eyes are open wide, staring up at the veiled sky, through the shifting crowns of the trees that bow in the cooling wind.

The baby has no mouth. The baby won't cry. We don't mind.

When she takes the baby from me we don't touch, or at least I don't have the sensation of her skin against mine. Maybe I wouldn't feel it even if we had. She is not quite smiling, my mother, I would say she looks resigned; everything she has seen since she left me is tied up inside her. She has the beauty of a statue, something imprisoned behind the stone, and when I wake I won't be able to imagine holding her close to me, just as I couldn't truly have been holding the baby. She takes it, the baby, and holds it, though its curled shape seems no closer to her body. The baby's mouthless face is turned away from me now, just the furred black crest of its head and her paper hands around its bound back as we begin to walk through the cemetery, but now there are no other stones. It is just a path through sparse trees, although the dead are all around us.

I don't ask her anything. If I ask the wrong question, she may disappear. I have wanted an oracle, but now that I'm with her I know she's not that.

Then she says: Here, poor thing. You're hungry, darling. Darling. I think she must be talking to the baby, but then I realise she is speaking to me. No one has ever called me darling before, at least not so it sounds like this. And she is breaking off bread and handing it to me, white pulpy stuff I would never eat if I had the choice but here there is no choice and it has to be delicious, the hunks of it my mother is breaking off for me and I am swallowing dry. The taste is thinner than air. The loaf of bread is in her arms where the baby was a minute ago, but I am not worried about the baby because I want the bread. The bleached swaddling around the writhing tiny body, the bleached yeasted cloud of the bread turning to nothing inside me.

I turn to look at her. The land is all gone, the trees, the air, I can see nothing but her, nothing. She is so close to me, she is not looking at me, I am looking at her and still the powdery bread is in my mouth, what have I eaten, what has happened? She won't look at me. She walks and walks and I walk beside her. I see she is weeping, not making any sound. I am thirsty. I stop, I take her shoulders in my hands and I try to lick the tears from her cheeks.

CHAPTER EIGHT

Tom woke in the night, aching. He had lain himself down between two blankets on the flags by the fire; now the warmth had long gone. She had fallen asleep almost as soon as she'd got into his bed, in her clothes under a sheet and his third blanket. Afterwards he had fished in her bag for the keys to her car and gone out to find what else might keep her warm: a duvet, which it didn't surprise him to find. He laid it over her, the keys slipped back into her bag. He did not look in her wallet, nor in the little black diary bound with elastic he found there. Janet: that is what she had given him, and he would not take any more. Not yet.

He didn't move for a while, almost relishing the force of the stone against his shoulder. He had been curled on his side. He lay flat, then, allowing his back to stretch, one hand under his head, staring up into the darkness, the shadowy roof-beams studded with the sharp iron hooks he couldn't see now, but which he knew were there. Outside the sea exhaled, inhaled, and the woman was breathing in the bed.

All those slamming doors. He had never cared. Never really wanted what they offered, never really noticed when they went. Why? One after the other, the women, they told him he was lazy. He was not lazy. He was the very opposite of lazy, and that is why they left. They offered, he took, he was good at taking, he was thinking of other things. That offering, hot as loss. He stretched himself in the cold and made a memory, a gathering of moments that might have been moments of tenderness. Sweet, salt, slick, the dampness of his own hair at the nape of his neck, or a curve of shoulder and a kiss. Then it was gone in the cold, it was his own breath he heard – no, it was hers, this woman, the sleeping woman, who had come here and claimed this place as he had always known she would.

He had unlaced her boots. She had watched him, her right hand gripping the iron bedstead, her knuckles white. She was rage, she was exhaustion, she was the question, she was the answer. Watching her from the path, the two of them watching the pair of seals. Her ignorance of him. He had felt this only once before, only once, the cleaving he'd known when she'd faced him on the path, her dark eyes, her dark hair, her fine, pale face. Her heel in his hands, her socks a little damp, the smell of her skin. He had known it before. It was the taste of a promise in his mouth. He held his spine still against the stone, his eyes were open very wide, and he matched his breath to hers.

* * *

I don't like it, he says. I don't.

He never complains. He has learnt to accept; he has learnt a different way to fight. But this is different. Something is different here.

They are standing in the stone house, the cold stone house that is empty as a cave, no, not quite, but seeming emptier for the single broken chair, the bedframe with its wild wire springs gone to rust, thick nests of cobwebs, spiderwebs, dead flies along the sills of the small windows. Some of the glass is broken, he sees a shard of glass on the floor. She doesn't seem to notice. She is looking up, all around, she is not holding his hand; he wishes she would hold his hand. He looks up to follow her gaze and sees the iron hooks in the beams of the roof, what are they for? He doesn't like them. It is cold in here although the day is warm, the place is cold with disuse and with its own sense of separateness which he feels, he feels clearly, though it will be years before he names it, knows it, banishes it at last.

Please, he says. He is about to cry. She can hear it. She whirls toward him, her skirt whipping against his legs, and then he is in her arms again as he was in the lane, only it's better now, his arms are around her neck, she's kneeling on the ground in front of him, holding him tight.

Don't be afraid, she says. *There's nothing to be afraid of* here. *We're home*, she says.

Tom will remember it, this feeling of dread. He will remember its conquest, too. He doesn't understand, *home*. Truly, there has never been home. He has been to other people's homes, sometimes, when he's had friends, or when someone's mother somewhere has taken pity on him and there has been warmth which does not reach him, which he can observe but never possess, the warmth of a single place, of a simple knowledge. He is careful to throw it off, far from himself, before it fills him with fear. So there is fear, here, when she says, *home*, in this place. How old is he? He never knows, he never remembers, not in that way – only he is sure he is too big to be held this way, like a little baby, rocked by her as his tears pool in the hollow of her throat and wet her hair and his nose is buried in the sweet shell of her ear, she is soft against him, soft, soft, closed against him.

Look, she says. *Look*. She takes his face in both her

hands, his wet face, drawing it away from her shoulder, her neck, he can feel the tears in his eyelashes when he blinks, blinks, blinks. Look at what? He looks at her, in the deep black of her eyes. It is dim in here but her face is lit, he is trying to take it from her, to share it, this mysterious delight she appears to feel. She is trembling with it as she holds him.

Come on, she says. *You're cold.* She rubs her hands swiftly up and down his arms. She's grinning, her white sharp teeth, one eyetooth, the right one, pushed forward as it always has been, almost like a fang, she's grinning and she nearly lifts him off his feet with her effort to warm him and then he's grinning too. In the rubbish of this place there are some sheets of yellowed newspaper, trashy wood, sticks, hardly kindling – though he didn't know any of this then, this was the first time he'd seen a fire built and he'd never have guessed that she knew how to build one – which she gathers and places by the stone hearth. Briskly, she rises, he follows, she knows it here, the way she walks confidently (afraid, afraid, afraid, his footsteps on the stone flags say) through a wooden door, a dark little room with a broken window, more cobwebs, more damp, he doesn't want to breathe, he is holding on to her skirt. But there outside, where the wind bucks suddenly against them and nearly throws him against the wall, there is the end of a pile of logs, tumbled down and silver with age. She gathers an armful, and then (he holds his breath again) they are back by the hearth, she is kneeling.

There are tiles around the fireplace: blurry figures with boats on their feet. Later she'll tell him they are Dutchmen – and women. The tiles come from Holland, where they hold the sea back with dikes. Their little blue faces out of focus, standing there by the fireplace, long in the past.

Her hands are dirty, now. Paper, twigs, wood. She is

humming under her breath, he knows the rise and fall of the tune although she is not singing the words –

One evening as I rambled
amongst the springing thyme
I overheard a young woman
enquire for Reynardine –

Her hands are so sure! It's like a magic trick. It's different from the certainty he sees in her fingers when she lights a cigarette or runs her bone comb through her hair. She makes a pyramid. He is standing close against her, so close he almost stumbles when she leans away, digs in her bag for her lighter. She hands it to him.

Here, she says. *You do it.*

He's not allowed fire, of course, though he loves the leaping flame. Her thumb on the flint, the quick breath of the gas, the metal lid open like a mouth. The explosion of a lit match even better. The bright, transforming, forbidden fire.

He takes the lighter. It's heavy. He knows what he has to do, he's seen her do it so many times, his thumb to press down, to turn the little wheel, to let out the blue-orange flame. But he can't. It's stiff. He tries, and tries again. She's watching him, until she reaches out her hand and curls it over his so their thumbs are joined to make a single pressure. Then the click, and hiss, and leap. Then their two hands, one hand, one arm, reaching the flame down towards the hearth where it takes and jumps. (Later, later, years later: still the sensation of her fingers curled around his as he reaches forward, again and again, with the light.)

Slowly, the warmth begins to reach them. The logs glow, the bark burning to a crust, falling away in scales, smouldering. Her arm around his shoulder. It's only afternoon but it feels later, here in front of this fire she's made. She wipes her hands, one against the other, brushing them together, though it doesn't make much difference. Still, humming through her teeth, the same tune:

Her hair was black, her eyes were blue,
her lips as red as wine
and he smiled as he looked upon her,
did the sly, bold Reynardine –

Neither of them hears his step, though it must have been what she is waiting for.

* * *

The woman was dreaming. Janet. He stood over her. Bending down close in the darkness, he could see her eyes moving behind her closed lids, this way and that, as if she were lost in a forest and was seeking a path through the hidden green. He did not recall rising so his feet were planted beside the iron bedframe, but here he stood. The taste of metal in his mouth: metal or blood. He swallowed, and it did not go. Her white throat, her long hair spilling from its plait, spread out on to the pillow. The shadows under her darting eyes.

She kept still when he touched her. He liked that. Only her eyes opening, but her body holding itself, like the stillness that comes after nightmare, when the mind takes the body prisoner to keep it safe. She could have shaken, or shouted, but she did neither as a lock of her hair wove between his fingers, as he felt the curve of her skull. Open eyes, following him. Open mouth, breathing. She might be wondering if she had woken at all, if this was sleep-vision, illusion, apparition.

His knuckle at her jaw. Then her head turned, to push him away, to draw him in. He cannot know. Then she spoke.

'What are you doing?' she said. 'You're making it worse.'

'What could be worse? What is there to be worse?'

'Nothing,' she said. 'There's nothing. Get away from me.'

'How can I?' He had knelt down by the bed. Now he wasn't touching her, but he was closer, closer to her. A synthetic smell, apples, from her hair. 'You came to me. Here you are, in my house.'

He could see how they struck her, those words, like a blow, *in my house*. Her eyes sparked to argue and then died back, so the flame in them was replaced by a different flame. What was it? The understanding of her own choice? The two seals in the water, two pairs of eyes and two pairs of eyes, and this woman observed, observed in silence, lying now in her clothes in his bed with dried blood curdled in her palm.

Again he matched his breath to hers. He felt his own skull move under the muscles of his face, the hinge of his jaw. Was he smiling, did he smile? She was not smiling. He reached out and put his palm on her shoulder; he could feel the bone, the ball of the joint. He could feel her rejection of fear, that is how it was to him, how her silence was not fear and was not acquiescence, either, but was a strand laid parallel to his own silence, a strand of electricity and intent.

All those women. This woman. The first woman, here in this house, her smoke-scent, her velvet, his wish to capture her as he'd captured animals, mice, frogs, burrowing in the hedgerows – but the things would die, that was the danger of capture, if you were not careful, if you did not let them go, they would die. A soft cage, a good cage. He wanted to explain something to Janet: he did not wish to use words. He wasn't sure what words he would be able to use, to tell her what he'd seen in this house, when he had first come here, when he was a boy. How he hadn't heard the stranger's step, but understood who it was as soon as he saw the mirror of his own face, his own wild pale hair, in the stranger who stood on the threshold. He imagined the woman (his mother, *his mother*, those were words he hardly ever chose for himself) looking into that face and seeing the mirror too. Her boy, that boy's father, this place, this old house. Once she had made her return and now Janet, unknowing, had returned too. The mirrors of the next generation. He would not explain with words. She would not understand these words. He would make her understand another way, see how he was possessed, and then she would come to that possession too.

Here was her mouth. Very close. Her chest rose and fell in the darkness, fast, fast, but she had moved her left hand, her injured hand, away from her body and raised it over her head.

He believed this was an invitation. His own mouth moved down over hers, the scrim of the sheet against the skin of his throat, his touch on the soft flat of her arm to hold her, and he felt her start, though she knew this would come. Why had she arrived here otherwise? Look what she knew, look at her key, look how she belonged here and belonged to him and to this place. He believed that if the knowledge was not in her mind, the knowledge of what she truly was to him, it was in her body. Her body that was his and that belonged to him because they were the same, of the same flesh, the same blood. There was no transgression in that. There was the righting of a wrong, the repair of a loss. That was the voice in his head, his own voice, as he opened her mouth with his own mouth and felt the edge of her teeth against his tongue.

She made no noise. He saw himself do this, kiss her. What had he meant when he had said to her, I am not a

132

thief? What was this, this kiss, if it was not theft? It was not something done with permission, the daylight permission of the words which say, in ordinary time: Yes, come in. Take off your coat. Sit down. Be welcome. Be welcome into me. But that was not how it had to be between them. The permission of his birth and hers, his arrival and hers.

No daylight here. Darkness and flesh. Something wet. Her tears. He pulled away.

He could not see into the depth of her eyes. They were dark hollows, each a wet abyss, infinite. He knew nothing of what she had left or where she had travelled to, though he would tell himself that there was everything here. In the quiet. In the soft black. In this shallow bed. What he would need to know, what he could teach her, what she could teach him.

He had never known desire. Every face passing before him, in his memory, and it was not this. It was not this.

* * *

He said my dear if you ask for me
perhaps you'll not me find
for I'll be in my green castle –

That tune again, and her arms tight around him in the webbed shadows. The smell of this old place in his nostrils, why didn't she mind? She liked to make it clean and new wherever they went, she would roll up her sleeves, there would be white paint and sometimes yellow, if she could, if they let me, she'd say, if they let us, bringing him into the secret. He liked her secrets. Then it would be theirs, the room, the flat, bedsit.

This place is not theirs. It can't be. This place is rackety, dirty and queer, the stone flagged floor so cold and streaked with earth, and there now on the ground is the bag full of blackberries, the juice seeping through the paper. It seems so long ago they were in the lane, picking the fruit, and Tom was wondering when he would eat it, what they would do with it. If there is something to eat there is nothing to be afraid of: he learnt this long ago, or learnt to make this equation with himself. It turns out there are more than blackberries: in her bag, wrapped in greaseproof paper, there are two pies with sturdy crusts and cold meat inside. They crouch by the fire and eat and he can imagine they are in the story he tells himself sometimes for comfort. He hardly notices how the two stories fit together, this one that is occurring right now, and the one he keeps in his head. In his head there is a story (he calls it that, but it is not a story, it is a pattern, a frame to hold himself against) of travelling. Someone travelling, and it might be him and it might not be him, but in any case there is a resting place and there is food and there will be sleep, the sweet trick of sleep.

He's with her, he's not with her. He is safe with her, he is safer without her. How does he know what is permanent and what is not?

She breaks apart her pie with her thumbs, catching a chunk of meat and fat before it falls on her skirt. He has finished what he has eaten and is still hungry, she can see that, she is smiling, her thumb and finger holding the meat, the fat, reaching out for his mouth, and he eats, her fingernail is smooth against his bottom lip.

Come here, she says. *Come close.* The floor is dirty. She doesn't seem to care. He doesn't care. He leans against her shoulder and closes his eyes and lets the fire's heat become him. Her black hair caresses his face and their greasy fingers twine together, this familiar knot that he loves, that he will lose, that he will never forget. I don't like it, he'd said, but perhaps he thinks differently now when they are, he knows, so far from anywhere and he can be here quietly, entirely hers, listening to the music that comes from her throat and dies away. Her music laps against him like the waves lap against the shore outside the splintered door, down towards the shingle, the freezing sea.

Wait, she says, *wait* – and then, *I forgot* – she is smiling. She licks her fingers clean and then takes his wrist and licks his too – *I forgot to bring napkins*, she says. Her quick tongue is neat. It tickles. His fingers are not much cleaner and neither are hers but still she digs into her bag and pulls out a little tube with a black cap she works off with her thumbnail. Inside is a bottle, a tiny bottle, the perfect size for holding an important message you would throw into the ocean, but there is liquid inside, the bottle must be emptied first. She unscrews its cap, breaking the seal, the splitting metal clicking against the spit and click of the fire.

She drinks from the bottle. It's different than drinking from a glass; it's like a potion. She licks her lips and looks at him.

Do you want to try? she says. She reaches out her hand and runs it through his hair, along his face. *Such a little man*, she says. *Such a dear one.*

He looks at her. The word that comes into his head is: together. So he nods. She hands him the bottle and he sees the light from the fire dance through it. It is green glass so he can't really tell the colour of the liquid inside. The tiny mouth of the bottle against his lips, and then the liquid on his tongue which makes him cough and spit, it is hot as the fire, though it isn't hot at all, but it is, it tastes like burning earth. She is laughing and her hand is on his neck. She pulls him close again, he is still coughing as she takes the bottle back from him and drinks again. Maybe not yet, she says.

He wonders if he should say: Thank you. He suddenly wonders if this wasn't some kind of trick, and thinks of pulling away from her, but he cannot. It is good here, against her. Quick cold in the marrow of his bones, the cold of doubt, and then it passes like wind blown through a door.

Wind blown through a door. An open door. The wind makes no footstep, but still the wind must walk through the world. Neither of them hears his step, though it must have been what she is waiting for.

She would have shrieked, cried out, but too fast does he have that hand over her mouth, from the corner of his eye he sees those broad fingers, bare and blunt-nailed, rough pale hair, and only much later would he remember that there was no scent from him, the stranger, nothing: as if nothing clung to him, or could keep him. And Tom, before he knows what he does, is on him, trying to claw some sort of hold while the fire shrinks back against the wind from the flung-open door, or tries to escape up the chimney, under their heels the fragments of pie crusts are crushed into the dirt and now the little green glass bottle smashes too, and soon everything will break.

There is a grip on his neck, on his arm, pulling him away, and he is trying to see her face, look at her eyes, is she afraid? They are savage, her eyes, in the light left from the fire, wide open, and her mouth open too now that the stranger has freed her and turned his attention elsewhere. He is laughing, the stranger, as she had laughed when he'd drunk the burnt earth.

This is the one? The stranger says. *This is the one?*

* * *

Janet did not move. It was cold. There was no fire. The only warmth would come here, here. Her open eyes and her stillness. Their faces a palm's breadth apart and he could taste her breath, a little sour, her lips dry, a white fleck of saliva at the corner of her mouth. He put his mouth over hers, again, and pressed, and judged the pressure of her – it was not resistance, it was not that. He opened her mouth. He sought her tongue with his own and here it was, soft, warm, the beginning of yielding. His fingers rested against her skin inside her elbow, just beneath her pushed-up sleeve. Under the pressure of his weight as he leant down towards her he felt the two bones in that arm, the sinew running between them, the quick blue vein that traced down into her wrist.

She shook. He would still her with his caress. It did not matter who was choosing, whose will was obeyed: this was not a place of choice. He drew her tongue into his own mouth and sucked it as he would a thumb, a nipple, a prick, and she made a sound in her throat as she let herself be pulled in, no words; drawing on her tongue, he would steal her language from her and give her back his own. When he moved his touch to her breast, when he began to work at the buttons on her shirt, he let go her mouth and tipped her head back with his chin. Now his mouth was on the pulse at her throat, tasting the salt in the hollow there, some memory of perfume.

Her dark eyes in darkness. Her flesh was known to him, his mouth against it, kissing her, devouring her. What was different about this, why was there no void here, the always-emptiness of the connection never made, despite hunger and sweat and the drugs of wine or music or violence? No void, a valley, the valley of this woman still cold in his bed, who had come here and let herself be split open, had already given him her blood. She would let him take the rest, the buttons of her shirt opening and he did not see how one dropped to the floor, scuttling away, thread curling off like smoke, her T-shirt underneath and he pushed it up, pushed it up to get at her breasts, which were round and high, and now she had put her head back and a stranger at the door might have thought she was in pain.

'I,' she said. 'I . . .' Her voice floated away from both of them, and he rose up to her mouth again to take her, her *I*, her assertion of presence, into himself. She was not *I* and he was not *he*, here, and there was no *they*, there was only this, this presence between them. Moving up to her bandaged palm, tasting the gauze and the blood and pressing fast with his mouth so she cried out and that made her put her arms around his ribs, one wrist cocked back, but she held him as if he would change or disappear if she did not hold and hold. She was fighting along with him, now, helping him as he dragged cloth away from skin until he could run his mouth into the ridge of her hip, the down on her belly raised against the cold, the drift of fur that ran towards the sweet heart of her, where even in this cold there was warmth. The thin sheet against the back of his neck, the top of his head, as he opened her legs and kissed her, the crest of her, the beginning. His teeth on her and she cried out, dragging at his hair now, his too-pale hair in her strong unwounded fist so that he was hurt and held her and would not let her go.

He would not let her go. The dead fire, black and grey ash, the hard stone floor, the night and the cover of darkness remaining with them for this, for him. He held her open now, her hips, her knees, the covers had slid off the bed and she twisted under him, biting at his shoulder, at his neck.

Why was this? Desire or recollection, recollection or

desire, and he could not have answered for himself in this close stone place, where he, the trespasser, yet belonged, and where he was a trespasser again as he entered her, her wet heat surrounding him, the arch of her back, her neck. He had turned her to lie on her front so she would close around him tight, tight, his breath in her ear, his teeth there on soft flesh and cartilage, trespass, transgression, permission. Belonging here, with this flesh, no space between them now, the flesh that as he moved inside it seemed to sing: his own, his own, his own.

* * *

And somehow there is a bed, not a bed, blankets, Tom will remember that. Enough of a bed so that when it is dark and he is afraid of the stranger it is good anyway to close his eyes against that gaze and sleep. He can travel in his sleep away from here, far from here, and no longer see her lit, furious gaze follow the man as he moves in the small room, as she watches him collect the broken glass from the smashed whisky bottle, throw the shards in the fire which he builds up again, more tinder and blown sprays of driftwood. There is candlelight; there had been candles in her bag. He'd seen her draw the candles out. Curled up in the blankets, which were damp and smelled of old things and maybe dogs, which he didn't like, he watches her light the candles, remembers how good the meat pies had tasted and thinks: This is not an accident.

The stranger takes Tom's chin into his hand: the fingers are strong and rough and cold and the stranger's eyes are the colour of his own eyes, dark sea-glass.

You left me, the stranger says. Tom doesn't understand. He didn't leave anyone. But he realises, in a moment, that the stranger is not talking to him, he is talking to her, although he keeps on looking into Tom's eyes.

I came back, comes her voice.

Twice you left.

And twice returned.

The stranger lets go of Tom's face and he scuttles back, near to the fire, feeling dust and sand under his palms, creeping into his clothes, before he can be captured again. It had felt like capture, held by that gaze and that grip, and he listens to them speak, his mother and this stranger. It's as if he's heard the words before because they are so like the stories she's told him, told him and told him all these years. It doesn't surprise him that she has this power to make the story live, to have one body and then another. This is why he knew he was in those stories. The stories, of course, were true.

You went so far, says the white-haired man. You crossed the ocean. To get away from me?

Yes, she says. Is she weeping? She is weeping. Tom would hold her but knows he must not, must not move, must keep still as a hunter, watch like a hunter, remember what he hears now all his life as the hunter will recall tracks and scent, will make those tracks and scent a part of himself.

You knew I couldn't cross an ocean. You know I am only here.

And here I am again, she says. *I told you. I returned. And look, look what I brought.*

Their two faces shine in the flames as they turn and look at him, and Tom sees her reach out for the stranger's hand, sees him hesitate, sees him take hers, sees his mouth twitch, the lips compressed, as if words want to come and he won't let them. His mother's face lit by the flames and lit too from inside herself. He understands that the light in her face is not something he has ever given her, will give her.

Later, waking, he hears them. He is curled in one corner; and there, in another, he sees them. There are more blankets. He is frightened of the noise, and the movement, which looks like harm, but he knows that if he goes to her, if he grabs at the shockheaded stranger as he had before, it will be worse for him, and for her, too. He is certain of that. He lies there still, as still as he can, as still as hide-and-seek, his eyes wide, and tries to conjure the feeling of her arm around him, her voice saying *Come closer, sit closer to me*, the way it had been just the two of them in this old, cold place, the flames just for them, even the singed bitterness of the whisky in his mouth.

But now she is away from him, far away, although there are only yards between them. One candle still burns and throws the spectres of them up on to the wall in shadow. The spectres loom over the curled lump of himself in the pilling, dogsmelling blankets and then he finds he is biting his fingers hard in his mouth because this way he might discover that he still exists.

The dark head, the white head, there is hardly any sound, there is the rhythm of movement, that sound, that sound like someone is hurt or he is hurting her or she is hurting him, he can't tell which. In the darkness, the darkness that won't leave, that will enter him, he can't tell which.

CHAPTER NINE

Here, in a stranger's bed, the memory comes. On the bridge between consciousness and sleep, when Janet is lying there with the print of his presence in her flesh. This memory, of a small, dark swirl in the water. Not so long ago, not too far away, a thousand years ago, a thousand leagues. She had been leaning back against the unfamiliar slant of a hotel bathtub; it was late, after dinner. Only the two recessed lights above the sink were switched on; the little room had a warm, luxurious holiday glow. Lying with her arms flat on the porcelain sides of the bath, simply recalling the crisp skin of the seared seabass she had eaten, the caramel soft-ness of the tarte tatin. She and Stephen had planned this weekend a long time ago, thinking nothing of it – but now it was different, a marker for something, a setting-off point. Neither of them had said that, of course, and yet – as they sat held in their car which was held in the train which was held in the tunnel, drawing them under the sea – it had been quite clear.

Sections of the newspaper spread over the back of the car. You could hardly feel any movement in the tunnel; it didn't seem like you were travelling at all.

It was as if all their conversations were suddenly over-heard. Did he feel it, too? He was turning the pages of a magazine. His expression was calm. His expression was always calm. Who was listening? She had no newspaper. Her hands resting on her lap. Her hands resting on her belly.

Ting-tong. The announcements, first in one language, then in another. The sound of keys turning in ignitions. Stephen smiled. His hand, quickly, on her knee. The day's wide, white light.

He had come home from a short tour. She didn't even remember where; there were so many places. He played a great deal in Eastern Europe, now things were different there. He was always bringing little gifts of unusual meats in tins or rough, hand-painted china. The particular sound his violin case made when he set it down in the hall, so familiar. His embrace.

So simple and gentle. It had always been like that, and she had always felt that this meant – that this was meant. That they fitted together, the ease of it. She didn't have to think about how she opened to him, it was as if there were no entrance. Could she separate one night from the many, ask herself how it had been different? Her arms around his shoulders and his hand on her breast, his mouth kissing her throat, and they had fallen into their rhythm, their breath and their bodies rocking, rocking, rocking. Sleeping, waking in the night to see him sleep.

Nothing had felt different. Should it have felt different? Should she have known? You ought to know when such things began, when your own self split and made something new: only, perhaps that was the trouble, that you didn't, that you became *other* and never saw, never felt, until it was too late.

Too late.

After their dinner, they had walked for a while on the promenade that was still the focus of the little town. This was the kind of place that had once been grander than it was now; that had once aspired to – though clearly never quite achieved – consequence. There were tall wooden houses with elaborate shutters; now, in early spring, they turned their blind eyes to the street. The tide was out, far out, and the sands stretched away, glistening, under a curl of moon and a few scudding clouds. Janet had zipped up her leather jacket and was glad of the warmth of Stephen's arm around her shoulder.

'We'll come back here,' he'd said.

'We're already back here.' It was the second time they had come. The first, a little over a year ago; they had stayed in the same hotel.

'You know what I mean,' Stephen said.

'Are you happy?' The sea drawing away from the sands, drawing in again. A long breakwater of rocks, and in the distance the lights of some factory twenty miles down the coast. A tanker on the horizon, two.

'Of course,' he said. 'Are you?'

'Of course,' she said. 'We never talked about it, that's all.'

Why had she asked him? What if his reply had been different? She had opened a door but he had closed it. She should not be thinking of things this way.

'Some things decide themselves, don't they?' He pulled a little yellow box from his pocket; the small cigars he sometimes smoked when he was travelling. Never at home. A cheap plastic lighter. He took a cigar from the box and then stopped himself. 'Do you mind?'

She laughed. 'No. Here.' She took the lighter from him, and he cupped his hands around hers while she made the flame and they both tried to keep it from the wind. She liked the bitter scent of the smoke in the salt air, and the unaccustomed taste it gave his mouth; she remembered that and it anchored her. 'I'm tired,' she said. 'I want a bath.'

They had reached the northern end of the promenade. There was a little bridge that let a gully of seawater and mud run under it; beyond, a rocky escarpment that looked spooky in the moonlight. The houses above were closed until the summer, dark and silent, like the little beach huts that ran the length of the promenade. The beach huts had names that sparkled hope, even on a cold night: La Noisette, Petit Ours, L'Étoile. They turned, and two teenaged boys on skateboards swerved around them, the clicking of their wheels in rhythm with the sea. 'If you want to keep walking, I don't mind,' she said.

'No,' he said. 'Let's go back.'

'No, really,' she said. 'You go on.' She wished to insist. To test his compliance, perhaps. To set that test in the guise of brief, companionable separation. She could have said that she wanted to show that distance was no distance, that an hour apart, even at the end of a delicious evening – especially at the end of a delicious evening – meant that the two of them were, somehow, closer together than if they had kept in each other's company. That is how she would have told the story, but that story would not have been the truth. He would go, or he would follow, it was her choice. She wished he would choose, and she wished to be alone. Her sense of the smoke-taste of his mouth faded.

'Maybe,' he said, 'I'll have a drink.' There was a hotel on the promenade – their hotel was just behind, on the main street of the town – which had a glassed-in bar that looked over the sea. They stood outside it, now. There were a few guests within, two solitary men and a couple twenty years older, perhaps, than Janet and Stephen. A waiter in a green-striped waistcoat was cleaning the espresso machine behind the sink. It was not yet ten o'clock.

'That sounds like a good idea,' she said. 'A cognac, with your cigar.'

'Armagnac,' he said.

'Whatever.' He kissed her, lightly, on the mouth, not touching her with his hands. His eyes creased at their corners with smiling.

'I love you,' he said.

'Me too,' she said. It was what there was to say. She laid her hand flat on his chest, briefly, then pushed him, smiling, both of them smiling, away.

The narrow streets were deserted as she walked back to the hotel. The modern houses had metal shutters that rolled down over their windows, and yet somehow the place didn't feel boarded up, as she was sure it would have done back across the channel of sea running between her and home. Home: the foreign place she had decided to possess for reasons she liked to tell herself were mysterious, but certainly they were not. Home, because the one thing that had kept her bound to what was an ocean away from her was gone now. Nothing was the same. Never mind. Now there would be something new.

Overheard. Who is listening? Who?

She didn't close the curtains in the room; it was not overlooked. Streetlight, a little moonlight, slipping in, further patterning the patterned carpet. She believed she was more sensitive to smell, suddenly: Stephen's cigar and that scent of butter, perhaps it was butter, as she had climbed the stairs. Monsieur Boulanger, at the reception desk, nodded at her as he passed her the room key with its heavy brass ring. Folding her clothes neatly, laying them on top of the suitcase, the sound of running water. The bath had Jacuzzi jets.

The unfamiliar – but comfortable – slant of the bath. The

heat on her skin. And then that swirl, not a beginning, but an end, the little darkness from between her thighs.

* * *

The Christmas before Stephen, I go home. Of course this is *home*, what else would it be? The apartment, the river, the bridge, the city, the deli on the corner, the old factory buildings that they're turning into lofts, but still they're there, the buildings persist. A taxi from the airport, no one meets me, I am a grown-up and can pay the fare and the tolls and tell the driver how to go. This high, bright, cold weather, how I miss it! Rolling down the window of the cab to let the bitterness batter my face. Escape from the bleak, leaching winter I have left behind across an ocean; the chill I can never quite become accustomed to, that drills into my bones and exhausts me. Dark in the morning; dark in the afternoon; the north. Who would think this city, the city where I was born, is a southern place? But it is, its towering buildings glittering in sunlight even at the turn of the year.

I have my own key.

He is sitting at the table (not the kitchen table, not the dining room table: there is only one table that is 'the table'), doing the crossword puzzle. He has a particular pencil for this, a particular eraser; he saves each puzzle, from day to day, cut out of the newspaper. This way he can check the answers.

His glasses perch on the end of his nose. My hand on his back. How familiar its curve, though it is more curved now than it used to be; and his thick hair is grey. Benjamin Nicholls Ward. He looks up at me, then quickly back down at the puzzle, smiling.

'"It goes up when it comes down",' he says.

'Um. Letters?'

'Eight.'

'Got any?' There's my chin on his shoulder, so our faces are side by side. The grey and black squares of newsprint.

'Em,' he answers. 'Ay.'

I got up at 4 a.m. this morning to catch the plane, but now I'm not tired, slipping back into the comfortable space here, always vacant for me. 'Umbrella.' I remember and always will. Umbrella.

'Excellent.' Capital letters. His distinctive M, a slant line and a little tent beside. The W is the same, reversed. Soon, I will sew these things into the hem of memory. 'All that private education. Worth every penny.' And then he stands up, and hugs me, my head against his chest and his mouth on my hair, just the same as always. Taking his glasses off, slipping them back into the little metal tube they live in, everything always ordered, in its place, so everything is safe, so I am safe.

'They said your plane was on time.' He goes into the kitchen, making coffee, not asking, knowing. 'Janey, it's so good to see you. You look good.'

'I feel good. I feel good to be here.'

'Do you want something to eat?

'In a bit. We could go out?'

I unpack. There is still my chest of drawers, bright red, in my old room, in the closet: he dismantled it and reassembled it to get it in there. In my head I know the vanished archaeology of my old clothes, how what I wore and how I tried to shape myself was once layered through those drawers, which are now mostly empty, though in some of them there is still an old sweater or two, or some things of his, reams of paper, an empty carousel for slides. Everything I've brought I could fit into one drawer, but I spread it out over two. Leaving the closet I see on the doorframe the pencil marks, each one dated, my height from year to year to year. The last one at the level of my eye. Was there a time when I knew I was too old for that? Of course not: a marker unmarked. Change like water, flowing away but looking the same.

Later, we walk out together, on those sidewalks, the brownstone houses with their tall stoops, the bare trees penned in by metal and cement, the shining door of the fire station. It's cold, of course it is, freezing – Dad has a red scarf tied tight around his neck, and a woollen cap pulled down over his ears. We walk down first to the promenade and sit down on a bench, the same bench, the always bench. The river is the colour of steel and the great bridge arches over it, stone and metal, quite alive. Cars and trucks hum over its span, a tugboat trundles through the water below, towards the sea. It's taken us longer to get here than it has before, I think; my arm tight-wound through his and now our gloved hands clasped together as we look over the water.

'I thought you might come with – what's his name?' he says at last.

What's his name? What could his name have been? There's no one. There hasn't been anyone for a while.

'Who, Dad?'

'You talk about him. Nick. Nick, isn't it?'

Nick co-ordinates the youth work at the small arts centre where I used to be the administrator; now, somehow, I'm the director, though that might sound more important than it is. Nick makes good coffee and good jokes, and I know that he goes to church on Sunday. No one else I know does that, unless they are trying to get their kids into a school. Sometimes I've thought I'll go out with him, but I haven't

149

told him that and I don't know, frankly, if I ever will. I laugh.

'I like Nick, Dad. But he's not. He's not. He works for me. He's a cool guy. But that's all.'

'Janey, baby.' He looks at me. He's embarrassed. My memories are a deck of cards, fanned or shuffled, scattered at our feet or tucked into my pocket. Why is he embarrassed? Because of what he wants for me. 'I just – it's so good to see you. You're not –'

I don't know. I'm not, what? 'Gay?' I try. 'Not recently.'

He shakes his head, laughing. 'I'd tell you if there was something important,' I say.

'I don't want you to be lonely.' The wind comes hard off the river, slaps us both. Suddenly I want to be inside, I want something to eat.

'I don't want to be lonely either,' I say. 'Dad, I'm not.'

'Okay,' he says. 'I'm sorry.'

'Dad,' I say. 'Are you?'

He looks away from me. At the metal railing, at the water, at the other skyline, at absence. Whatever is on the opposite shore. The opposite shore, anywhere. The crossing you can't make. I have never asked him this question before. This is the truth. All my life. Have I ever wondered? I don't know. I don't know. I don't know.

He does not answer me. He keeps his gaze on the river, and he keeps tight hold of my hand. The cold has made the end of his nose red, and perhaps it's the cold that's rimmed his eyes red too. I should get him inside, I think. He is old. Inside my head, I take that back, and amend it: he is not young. Not any more.

Suddenly my mind takes me to another shore, a beach one summer Sunday, a long, long rolling stretch of the ocean. Was it truly empty of anyone other than us, or is it only my thoughts that have made it so? My father running, running, holding a red kite with a snapping tail aloft, the soles of his bare feet, the thread unspooling and unspooling in my hands and the undying sun on my face.

His gaze fixed on the river.

'Let's go get lunch,' I say.

* * *

It is the memory of what she thought she could have, what her body abandoned: when Stephen returned, Janet had got out of the bath.

'Janet?'

She was sitting, with a towel wrapped around her, at its edge.

'What is it?' He fills the doorframe. She can smell the smoke on him from here. It seems so long ago, that they stood on the promenade in the dark and their mouths touched.

She stood, and there was an oval of blood on the towel.

There was nothing to do, though they must do it. She had brought nothing with her that she might have needed, of course; together they dressed and went out to the little supermarket that was, fortunately, open until midnight and bought pads, not tampons, although she hasn't used a pad since she was twelve. But she did not want to put anything inside herself, not yet. To her great surprise, that night, she slept, and slept dreamlessly, as if she had been anaes-thetized. Nothing came to her in her dreams, and whether or not Stephen lay awake beside her – she didn't know and, in the morning, didn't ask.

Monsieur Boulanger directed them to a small local hospi-tal. He didn't ask what the matter was. His brow furrowed, just a little, when she asked in that unfamiliar, decorative language where they might find such a place, but he was careful and kind. He even drew them a map. The place he sent them to was hardly a hospital, really: an infirmary, she would have called it. Strangely, when she passed through its swinging doors, Stephen's arm around her shoulder, and her footsteps rang on the linoleum, she remembered her summer camp in the woods, her fear of tennis lessons, the heat, the sweat, and how the infirmary, with its understanding nurse, had been a cool haven of books and Jell-O. This place seemed the same.

There was a single nurse, a single doctor and no other patients. Eight o'clock on a Sunday morning and everyone else in the region was healthy, why should they not be? The doctor was a compact man with broad, capable hands and a collarless shirt buttoned to the neck. He wore a pocket watch. He was serious, he was not unkind, and his English was stilted, heavily accented, and perhaps – Janet found herself thinking – this made him sound more solemn than he truly was. He did not examine Janet; she sat in a chair in a small white room near his orderly desk. A window high-set in the wall looked out over the parking lot where they'd left the car, askew over two spaces. She had imagined, they had both imagined, there would be sheaves of forms to fill in, but there was nothing, for there was nothing for the doctor, Dr Blondeau, to do. He sat with his hands resting on the creases of his trousers. Was he smiling? It was impossible to tell.

'I am sorry,' he said. 'Nature knows the way sometimes, even though it seems difficult. You are young. Don't worry. Take it easy. Try to enjoy the rest of your holiday. How long are you here?'

'Just until tomorrow,' Stephen said. There were two

chairs in the little consulting room; he had dragged them together and sat close to her, holding her hand.

'*C'est un beau jour,*' the doctor said. 'A beautiful day. Go for a drive. Have a good meal. You should eat properly.' He looked at Janet's pale face and now he did smile, certainly. 'And you should rest. That's all. You will be fine.' He looked at them both, this couple. 'It seems foolish to say but – there are always new beginnings.' A small, self-deprecating laugh. 'Forgive me, these are platitudes. You will begin to think I consider myself a wise man.' He rose, and so did they.

They shook hands, Stephen and Janet in turn with Dr Blondeau, formally, as the occasion seemed to require. As they turned their backs and walked down the corridors to the swinging doors that swept them from the low, ugly building, as their feet took them back to their car, Janet felt the pad between her legs and sensed a weight dragged out of herself – but then decided this was her imagination, over-active, overdramatic. She fastened her seat belt and propped her feet on the dashboard, the way she always liked to sit but which she knew irritated Stephen; she knew also that he would say nothing, this morning.

'Where shall we go?' he asked, turning the key in the ignition.

'"Go for a drive", he said,' Janet answered. 'It's funny. No one "goes for a drive" any more, like driving was a recreation. Or do they? They drive because they have to. They drive to get somewhere.'

'Well,' said Stephen, 'Let's try. Let's go for a drive.'

They did. It was not yet nine o'clock when they left Dr Blondeau; the spring morning sky was hardly blue, pale and high, new. Spring wasn't a story, or a cliché, it was simply true – and Janet was glad of it, it wasn't strange to her.

Something inside her had ended, and yet her emptiness was not a lack. Her feet up on the dashboard, she rolled the window down. It was one of her favourite things, a small pleasure, to be driven. She liked a long drive, she liked not to read the map, she liked someone else to get behind the wheel and go, so she could look out of the window, or tip her seat back and close her eyes, and the world would flow away from her, out behind her, out of her control. This was a good thing to do.

Primrose and violet, the colours of the sky. Its texture shifting as the sun rose, and laying patterns of light and cloud on the dusty green fields they passed, so wide and neatly ordered, tilting down towards the calm sea. Stephen drove on to the autoroute and then off again; she didn't ask what he was doing, where he was going. She didn't care. He looked peaceful, but a little tired, she thought.

'Are you okay?' she asked. She cared for him. This is what love was, it lived in this question, in another, and another after that. The wall of kindness was support. Whether it came easily or not – that didn't matter, that was not the point.

He glanced away from the road, at her, smiled. 'Yes,' he said. 'Yes. Sure. I'm – worried about you.'

'Don't worry,' she said. 'I'm fine. It's like he said. The doctor. It happens. I guess your body knows things you don't. Not always.'

'Yes,' he said. 'Yes.'

A small road leading into a village: the white and black sign with its name, a straggle of boxy modern houses becoming a sort of main street, with a bakery, a bar, a tobacconist's.

'I'm sort of hungry.' she said.

'Good,' he said. 'Me too.'

154

They went to the bar: it was the only place. She thought how, usually, when they travelled, they would expend such energy on finding the right place – somewhere with 'local colour' (the particular kind of 'local colour' they sought), or where someone had told them the pastries were especially good, some place that had whatever intangible sense that made them believe they were having the correct experience. You couldn't be lazy. You couldn't not think and simply set yourselves down in the first place you came across. But why not?

The bar was very ordinary – somehow this quality struck her as a kindness, just then. The gloss-painted walls were hung with ragged posters for stock-car races that had happened long ago; the paint itself was practically brown, stained with years of cigarette smoke. The man in a white vest and holey cardigan wiping down the bar nodded at them as they came in and sat. Stephen went to the bar and asked for coffee, and whether they could get anything to eat. The man nodded.

'He didn't say what there was to eat,' Stephen said when he sat back down. The barman brought the small, dense coffees and stood over them. He was neither smiling nor unsmiling. Janet thought of what the doctor had said, how anything seemed, this morning, impossible to determine. She did not mind, it was a kind of equilibrium. Waiting. Not knowing. There were only small decisions to take. That was all right.

Guessing, she asked for an omelette, and Stephen said he would have the same. Bread arrived, pale and soft and salty, and she broke a piece apart with her fingers and ate it. Her hands were on the table, so were his, they were sitting across from each other, not touching, their knees not touching, and it seemed to Janet that Stephen was looking at her as if someone had suddenly told him that she was someone else, or that she was made of something breakable. Was she breakable? This was not breaking her. Blood loss, something lost. And yet she did not feel it. She was hungry, and when her omelette came, a stalwart yellow on its white plate, a flourish of green leaves and chives beside it, she devoured it as Dr Blondeau had advised.

He was watching her. His face had sunk into itself. Did he look lost? What did that mean?

'It's good,' he said.

'Yes . . .'

Who was he, Stephen? How did she get here? She felt very calm. She was simply trying to remember something and it would not be retrieved because it was, somehow, too permanent, too much a fixture of herself, of both of them. If they had become each other, would she know herself any more? With Stephen she had accepted something, what he had wanted to give her. Whatever it was, he was always wanting to give it to her. Was that too much? What had she offered in return? She had the sense that she had tried to offer something and that had not been allowed. Nature knows the way sometimes, the serious doctor had said. Yet she was not relieved. Your life was a structure. You built it yourself and then you climbed, building as you went, higher and higher, until you couldn't see the base any more, couldn't even recall if you had used stone or brick or straw and mud. Stephen ate his omelette, here in this bar in a town whose name she didn't even know, posters on the walls that meant this moment in time could have happened years ago. The dark-stained wood of the table. The ring on the little finger of his left hand. It had been his mother's. They had never met, Janet and Stephen's mother; she had died when he was twenty-one, she had cancer, yet she had never thought of this as something they had in common. He had not been without a mother. There was his mother's ring on his finger.

To whom would she give a ring? She looked down at her naked hands and ate.

* * *

There are no papers relating to the death of my mother. No death certificate I can find, no hospital records. I don't even know what else there might be, newspaper clippings? It was a drunk driver that killed her. She had gone out to buy cigarettes – she smoked, yes, even with a baby, that baby was me, in the house. Did my father mind? I don't know, that isn't part of the story. She had gone out to buy cigarettes. The sideswipe of life. One moment changes into another moment, that's all, only everything is different. You will not know the moment when it changes. There will be a time when something awful has happened – maybe the moment you are my father upstairs, I am asleep, I am three, there is a siren, there are always sirens in the city of course, but they wail from far and move near and then go far again – only this one doesn't. She has stepped off the curb in the shadow of the bridge and been hit. Weaving taillights, the sound of her fall that would have been loud in a room but is lost in the night-time street. In the silence before the siren my father lives in the illusion that his life is the same. It is not the same. No one has told him, that's all. He is happy. He should not be happy. But he does not know.

This kind of thing happens all the time. It is an ordinary, terrible story. This is not the story to ask him for. I don't want details. Why should I? Why should he?

Luckily, when the stroke comes, it is easy enough to get

time off from work, to fly across the ocean, to come back to the place I was born and sit, for not so many days, in a hospital room holding his hand. He can't tell me stories any more, he can't speak, so I fill the air with nothing, with my days, the things I've never bothered to tell him because I have never had to fill this space. Where I like to get a bacon roll when the weather gets cold. The kid from the crap school over the river who's come in to volunteer, the bad jokes he tells. He doesn't like to leave at the end of the day, we know what's going on at home, we hang around with him a little drinking instant coffee and laughing. Easter holidays and he was there every morning before we unlocked the doors. Ahmed. What will become of Ahmed?

I don't call the office. I don't call – no, I hadn't told my father the truth, there is someone, but we don't know each other well, it's not serious (that's what you say, isn't it?) and so this is not his concern. Or maybe, I will come to think this later, I like these boxes of existence. One here, one there. Separation is safer than conjunction.

How things, objects, hold or lose meaning. Now I am alone in his apartment, our apartment, my apartment, with all his life, our life, my life, held in the web made by these objects. A Waring blender. A gyroscope. A matte knife. A pair of snowboots. None of it any good to anyone. I have got boxes, I am putting things in boxes. I think I will be overwhelmed by a desire to keep things, to hold them to me, to possess. But nothing offers consolation. Before my eyes the objects are leached of the qualities that made them a part of life.

But there are no papers. No newspaper clippings. It has never occurred to me to find out more than the story he always told me, the story he didn't want to tell anyhow, that had a siren, a hospital, a funeral, these bare bones of event. I never go looking for records or seeking evidence. I like stories. I believe stories. It is only later that I think of what I don't find, what is missing. What has always been missing. The truth.

I wind the string around the gyroscope and pull. I am sitting on the floor with the boxes all around me, the winter sun dropping down through the dusty windows. Sitting on the floor makes me remember playing jacks, my legs crossed, the little pink bouncing ball, its hypnosis. The gyroscope spins, swaying, balanced, blurred. A siren, a hospital, a funeral: now at last, I will know what it's like. There was no siren, not for me, unless you count the evening ring of a telephone, but that was just like any other phone call, it was not the heart-rush of the small-hours call, the wrong number, the emergency, that moves your blood with alarm. The click of the receiver: Hello? Any other hello, one hello out of so many. Bill Gatti, our downstairs neighbour. He had heard a thump. Thump.

A hospital is a machine, in one end and out the other. This is the hospital where I was born, I know that, I almost believe that will make it seem familiar to me, and very late at night, when I am still here, still here, uselessly, silently, by his bed and I am exhausted but there is no reason to sleep, I wonder if the linoleum corridors might not hold the stories it is too late to seek. Through plastic tubes and down the hollow metal legs of gurneys the stories are flowing away from my silent, dying father (I say that to myself, my dying father, my father is dying) and I cannot retrieve them, although I would crawl on my hands and knees to do so, would try to lap them up as they swirled down into the drains of this place, out into the city, underground, through pipes, the story of my life, his life, flowing away, and where is she? There she is, escaping again as she had escaped when

I was a baby, a girl. Hit by a car.

He was bereft, when she was taken from him. Killed. He had no words for that. There was only the future. He had me. There was no looking back. He runs on the beach and the long tail of the kite streams away from him, the cord spinning out from my hands so the wooden reel is hot against my palms, until finally the kite rises and rises again and its colours disappear into the face of the sun. His arm around my shoulder, tight. The salt ocean, where everything begins. A billion grains of sand drawn down into the sea, ingrained in my skin, I will never get rid of this, this sand, this clasp, this love.

I watch him breathe. Then he is not breathing. Then there are no more stories. Memory and breath, breath and memory.

Where did she go?

I am three years old.

Another hand on my shoulder, a stranger's hand. 'Miss Ward?'

* * *

So Janet had lain beside Tom, her mind captured by the past, by a moment, the moment when she'd lost the child she'd never known she wanted and something had changed, although she didn't know it at the time. No, not a child, it was not a child, it was too soon to think of it that way, it was an *it*, a *that*, something biological, a fact, not an emotion. Two decisions, conception and loss, that seemed to have been taken but without her knowledge or consent. The body's opening that accepts another so completely, the completion of creation. Then the body's abandonment, a shrugging off. How immense it seemed to her suddenly, although (hard to believe, but truly so) she had not given it much thought before. Because they had not been – as some of their friends were, as the dinner-party talk went sometimes, wincingly, unbearably – 'trying'. She, they, had been careless. Now she wondered if the carelessness was larger than that, or nothing to do with that, that lost child, at all.

Acquiescence. Quiescence. Quiet. It was quiet here, now. There was only the sibilance of the sea and the breeze in the marram grass and wild garlic, the lick and suck of lapping waves in the darkness outside. Her own acquiescence, a new kind of acquiescence, to this. To him, Tom. Was he asleep, this man? Lying beside her, stretched on his back with his eyes closed. Just enough light here so that his pallor seemed to glow; her own skin looked almost dark against his. The flicker of his closed eyes. She leant up on her elbow, feeling the stickiness between her legs when she shifted, less careful of her hand now, less caring. She drew the cover off him, but he did not move. White and straight as a body on a tomb. The shallow rise and fall of his chest that was smooth as a girl's. She rested her hand against it, her good hand, a gesture of curiosity rather than tenderness. She saw, she had not seen before, that he had a scar, a seam on his belly that jinked around his navel and ran right down to his pubic bone. Whiter against the white of him. She imagined him ripped open, and wondered who had done it, and why. Janet ran her fingertip along its line, lightly as she could, trying to read the smooth keloid tissue like Braille, as if it would give up its secret to her skin. When she reached the milky down above his prick, light and soft as dandelion seed, he put his hand over hers, so swiftly she didn't see his movement, started.

He opened his eyes. Such a clear, direct look, and she was frightened. Frightened because she was not afraid – not afraid of what had happened, or of what would happen, because she knew the path was marked now, somehow, and she could only follow it. The idea of explaining what had happened, what was happening, to Stephen flashed across her mind, the impossibility of it; the idea of explanation swirled away like blood. There was no place other than this place, now. She did not know why she knew that, only that she did, so when Tom spoke and said, Come with me, she did.

They rose from the bed and dressed, or half-dressed. He put on a shirt and sweater and she did the same; it was hard, dragging on her clothes with her bandaged hand, and she was cold too and tired, shivering a little but not minding, trying to make her body do as she bid it. He helped her, pulling her jumper down over her head. She reached for her jeans but then he was moving towards the door with his legs shining bare, the alabaster soles of his feet lifting off the stone flags.

There was no moon. Brilliance scattered out from the receding stars and their ancient heedless radiance stitched a cloak to cover them. He held her hand, her good hand, and she heard the door bang shut, unlocked, behind them, but did not turn her head. Stepped quickly because he made her and soon she was glad that her feet were so cold. She could not feel the stones which jammed into her flesh, though he kept away from the broken path, stayed at its edge, but the dune grass was rough and sharp against her skin, filing along the skin of her ankles, her legs. There was her car, though she could hardly believe it. The wind, at least, was low, and gentle, did not push but caressed, drawing itself kindly through her loosed hair.

It should have been silly, his naked legs moving through the land. It was not. Light from the stars, leaping back from the water, tipped the thorn trees, the gorse, with blue glow, so they walked in the negative of a landscape, the world dropping away into a silver print of itself. This vision of the two of them, heading down towards the water – she could tell that was where he took her – was a picture in a locked room away from anything else. She thought of the room in which she placed her seizures, that closed, dangerous, particular space to which all were denied entry except herself – only now there was another in that space, there was Tom. This place was the same as that room. That was why she could accept it. It was simply that she had been here before. She had always been given access, only she had never known to what. Now the knowledge, the purpose, was revealed, in the half-dark, half-light of starlight thrown back from water, the rush of the current, the rush of her pulse.

Down and down towards the rocks which made a natural wall before the sand began to stretch away, the tide, she thought, just drawing out. For a moment he let go of her hand, and they stood side by side, but he did not look at her. He looked out to sea, as if he sought something, as if he were waiting. It seemed to her he was always waiting for something, though how she felt this or why she knew it she could not have said.

They had been moving quickly and her blood had warmed, but now the slight wind in the damp air found a way into her bones and a shudder racked her so she nearly fell against him. Then he turned to her, only for a moment, and took her hand again and held it tight, so that their arms were nearly wound together, bone against bone. He kept her upright. He took her into himself (she thought) and steadied her. How could she have thought he steadied her, this violent stranger? But it was her own violence: she had brought it with her, sealed in herself, and he had only released it.

As she stood against him on this shore a word entered her mind. Her mother, she had come looking for her mother, some relic of what she was, what had made her. What had made *Janet*. Something had called up in Janet's mother a yearning for escape; yet she had understood that yearning as soon as she had put herself on the road, begun to drive into the dawn. A word entered her mind, here. It was not *mother*. It was near, but not that.

Not mother, but brother. *My brother*. Bone against bone.

She pushed the word away. It slid down over the rocks, ran down the sand, drowned itself in the sea. And then the seals returned.

CHAPTER TEN

Tom had called them and they had come. No, he had not
called them – it was not possible, it could not be. But as he
had lain next to Janet in the darkness and felt the drift of
her touch on his skin, even behind his own closed lids he'd
felt the strength of her dark eyes, and in that strength was
the recollection of those two glossy heads, those two sets of
eyes. The strength and recollection together made certainty.
He rose from the bed, drew her up too, dressed them both
just enough and took her out to the sea in darkness. The
new-moon night. Starlight. He had not needed to call them.
Of course they would be there.

In the moment before the seals' heads broke the surface
of the waves Tom and Janet stood together on the shore,
hand in hand, fingers wrapped tight, twined. Like children,
he thought, he had an image of them together there as children, at the beginning of an adventure, a mystery. A discovery. The discovery of themselves.

The breeze had picked up. It blew around his bare legs,
up his shirt, up hers, they shivered and clung and this queer
clutch at his heart was barely familiar or recognisable, but
in that instant he knew he must learn to call it content.
Happiness. The making of what had been broken whole.

'Look,' he whispered. 'Look.'

She had already seen, he was sure.

Not hard to see, if you knew how to look: the two dark skulls against the water's blackglittered fathoms, hidden bodies rocked a little by the sea's cold cradle. They did not flinch or slip away when he began to climb the rocks. A slight resistance in her grasp when he pulled her to the water, but the fear of falling was a simple fear and easily overcome. His toes curled around the rocks, shale pressed out of the aeon's mud and risen up into the air, and she followed him. Out of the corner of his eye he could see the white of her wrapped hand raised in the air, kept safe and used for balance, stretched outward, fluttering like a wing. Down past the rocks and then their feet in the firm freezing sand, he kept walking, kept walking, sure and certain; and she was with him, alongside him, as the first waves curled against their ankles, against their calves and knees, the water was as cold as broken glass. He heard her gasp when it hit her skin, like the noise she'd made when he'd held her against him, entered her, possessed her, the blown-out shock of the inevitable.

Tom let go of her hand and rose to dive.

The water burnt him with cold and bound him with iron, roared in his lungs, wrapped itself around him, a green serpent made of ice.

He heard her say his name. Tom, she said, Tom.

Four bodies in the water. Fur against flesh and flesh against fur, all without fear. He knew they were there; he was warmed by wonder as the heavy dense flesh of the seals rolled around them, not playful but serene. This was the moment when he knew the stories were true, the stories his mother had told him; that he had been right to come back here, right to wait. The moment of truth. You heard people say that, but it didn't mean anything; now it did. He saw Janet stretch out her arm, her foot kicked his shin as she trod water, he saw her stretch out her arm and the seal's side seek her caress. The quick vision of its onyx eye. Some caress against his thigh, dragged through the weight of the salt, and he could not tell if it was animal or human, would not want to know. The bitter salt was in his mouth, on his skin, and rinsed him clean. The grey seals, wakeful as their human companions in this brilliant, endless night, made patterns of infinity in the shifting sea, diving and diving again. And Janet's white throat, her head thrown back, the wild sound of her laughter.

Later he would come to believe he had dreamt this, and yet he would know it was true. Beneath the waves he took her hand again, her left hand, kissed it, in the cold sea he drew her hot blood into his mouth.

* * *

Years ago, Tom here in this place. Not the new moon, the full moon. The full moon and the second night in which they walk through the bluelit air, out along the edge of this place. It is the edge of the world. She has not spoken of their visitor; he has not spoken of what he has seen.

She knows what he likes best.

Tom sits on the coarse, prickly grass. The moon is as clear as the sun, huge, remorseless. Her skirt is a circle around her legs, over her drawn-up knees. He sits on its fabric and there is her embrace, her cheek against his hair, against his skin, the grip of her fingers on his arm that means, always means, that she will begin to speak.

He knows he will see her story, the story she is about to tell, here at the rim of everything. He knows it belongs here, on the barren plain at their backs. The wind lifts off the sea and takes her words up over the land.

Once upon a time, as long ago as never and near enough to now, a woman watched from the window of her father's house. No. Not a woman, a girl, older than you – fourteen. So – a girl watched from the window of her father's house –

Did she have a mother? His words floating in the air before them.

I'll never finish the story this way.

He is quiet.

Can I go on?

Yes.

The world as she watched through the diamond-paned glass of her window was broken in pieces; it was not enough. She remembered, as she watched, stories she had heard: stories about another place, but one that was her father's, too. A forbidden place. A place all in ruins, broken down and overgrown with briar, a place that had wanted to be a wilderness. Everyone who told the story would end by saying: do not go there. Never go there. Never, ever go. But the girl was a bold girl, after all.

Who told her those stories?

Her friends, she says. *Her friends. Her aunts, her cousins.*

He has no aunts or cousins, and not really any friends. He takes her answer in.

Don't go there, that was what they said. Everyone knew. Everyone knew that in this place there was a spirit, a thief, who –

She stops. He waits.

A spirit. He guarded this place. He was jealous. He owned nothing, but he believed he owned the ruined place. But the girl, she knew a different story. She knew this in her heart, that the ruined place did not belong to the spirit alone; though how her heart had come to the truth – she had no words for that. But she was quite certain of what was in her heart.

She didn't tell anyone she was going. It was midsummer day, the very longest day of the year, when the sun lingers on the edge of the world as if it can't bear to turn its face away. She walked out through the garden of white roses her father had planted; they were in full bloom, and she crushed a scatter of their ivory petals under her feet. It was morning, the sun was high, and she walked and kept on walking, following her toes, following her nose.

She had taken bread and cheese with her, wrapped in a cloth, and a flask of plain water from the well. But she didn't stop to eat. When she was hungry she ate as she walked, chewing to the rhythm of her step. It was a warm day, but not hot; she wore a wide-brimmed hat to keep the sun off her face. She did not grow tired. This was the world, and it was all before her. She felt the spring of the ground under her step; she passed by an orchard bright with apples not yet ripe but still leant over its wall to pluck one from a branch, a pair of magpies with their bold eyes on her as she did. The apple's flesh was sour and her mouth puckered and stung.

She walked across fields, over stiles, along green lanes and by the side of stone walls, and saw no one as she went – except once, in the distance, a figure on the crest of a hill, a figure that was gone as soon as she had looked. She thought she heard a dog bark, once, but it could have been the wind – which changed towards the afternoon, when the sun was beginning its reluctant progress into night. The girl lifted her head, sniffed the air, something salt and sharp.

The sea, says the boy.

The sea, says the storyteller. *She'd never smelled the sea before. Imagine that.*

The boy imagines, and the woman strokes his hair.

She smelled the sea, steely and bright as a blade. And then she rose over the crest of a little hill, and saw the sea – for the first time – broad, blue, green, full of fish and secrets, sparked, wild.

The pair of them look out at the sea, it is the same sea, honed under the moon's eye.

She saw the sea, says the woman, and by the edge of the sea, a house.

* * *

Tom and Janet had stumbled back up towards the house. There was a moment when the seals had disappeared, choosing to slip away into those comfortless depths. Tom was no longer cold, he felt bodiless, lifted and dropped by the current, pushed and slapped by the foam. But he could see that Janet's face was taut and chalky, the bridge of her nose showing sharply, the edge of her skull. Her eyes open wide but sunken. He'd reached for her, led her up as he'd led her down, kicking his legs and feeling her churn the water next to him until his feet found the gravelly land, their more familiar element.

The wind was a vice that grabbed them, nearly froze them still as they rose up out of the black water towards the black rocks and the path.

The fire long dead, and only each other for warmth. Wet cloth in the dark, indistinct from the puddles it made on the flag floor, water indistinguishable from blood. Her left hand was bare now; he could feel that the edges of the wound had tightened and puckered in the salt and cold, an illusion of healing. She shuddered against him, or did he shudder against her? There was no knowing. He couldn't have spoken, his teeth clenched shut, and rough with the residue of the sea and hardly dry they dived into the bed as they had dived into the water, and for a little while, arms wrapped tight around each other, naked, they slept.

In the dawn a rim of rosy light made the tiles around the fireplace gleam; he must be awake to notice that. The breaking day set a flush, like dawn, on her collarbone and breast. Her blood had left a mark, the mark of herself in his bed.

He did not believe in promises. He had heard a promise once – *I'll never leave you* – and that promise had been broken. Yet, for all that, he had come back to this place knowing that if he did she would, somehow, return; perhaps that was the certainty she had left him. Certainty in the shape of a lock and key, if she had left him nothing else. He had been right. She had returned. He was the lock. Janet was the key.

Now he did not need memory. Here was the present. Here was the curve of this hip, this breast, this belly, his hand on the downy hollow in the small of her back to hold her close to him as she awoke. He knew she would pull away, but her sweet wetness was here now, her blood, her self. There had been no tenderness in what he'd done before, but now with that black gaze fixed on his he reached down to her and curled his finger through the soft whorls, whorls soft as seal-fur, where she opened, where she began and ended. Her eyes closed and opened again; the thin skin at her temple trembled and the blood from her palm was on his back now, her arm over him, as she gave herself to this caress, the reparation for brutality that had only been the echo of her own. Folded and infolded on herself, could his fingers find some secret here, or here, or here? He sought her this way, and felt her leg hook up over his hip to permit him.

Her neck curved back, her eyes closed, her mouth

unsmiling. She did not seek to return his gesture and he was glad. He did not want her to. He observed her, her sensation, his vision of her. The singing salt of her, edged as the sea, her scent rising in him, her sweat, her sex, and he wondered, at her shuttered eyes, their flicker, who she imagined he was, or if she accepted him for what he was. He wondered what she knew and did not know.

Now she placed her right hand, her good hand, over his own, showing him where the depths of her lay, this opening, this speed, this slowing. Others, others had pressed close to him in their desire, but what he felt now was new and complete. His other hand closed on her breast and his mouth moved down to take the hard rosy crest between his teeth, to take it as he'd taken her tongue, hard into his mouth. Still her throat arched away, her eyes shut, even as her mouth opened and she made a sound which he told himself was the true sound of her. He heard again her laughter in the sea. If he never knew more than her name, he would have this, he would know this, and though he had never felt any longing for possession the knowledge of this possession rose in him wildly, the shape of joy.

But then something changed in her; a vibration that was not this crisis, the one he'd expected, the pitch and tilt of her pleasure though he had sensed the tip of that, her hand to guide him as she pressed against him, forced it out of herself like a birth. Not that – just after that – there was another shift away, a shudder, and now her eyes were open, there was fear in them, but he could see it was not fear of him. He could see she could not see him. She stared straight at him and straight through him and her mouth was an O, her skin white, and she receded from him like a tide. He could not have explained it except to say he was afraid she would disappear.

His hand up from between her legs, the moisture of herself on her own skin as he held her but could not keep her from vanishing. No, she said. No. She did not push him away but there was nothing to grasp, some electric darkness had hold of her and would not release her until it was done. His arms around her. Tight. Holding her warm flesh and the empty air, her hollow eyes.

Then it was over. She shoved at him, but then clasped at his shoulder as if she wanted to keep him. He moved a little away.

'Are you all right?' He heard himself say it. What else could he have said? It meant nothing.

Her eyes were wide and bright, full of tears.

'Yes.' It was as if he had never heard her voice before. 'It's nothing to do with you.' He did not believe this, either. I'll never leave you. 'It's nothing to do with you. I want – I want to sleep.'

He drew the cover up to her shoulder. Kissed her, though he had not known he would. Her mouth, her forehead. Then he left the bed, left her, curling up in the morning cold on the stone flags of his own floor.

* * *

The house is behind them, the house Tom and his mother have left. Even in the light of the full moon it cannot be seen from here; the path dips and curves and hides it from view. But it is the house he sees when she says the words, by the edge of the sea, a house. What other house can it be? He is cold now and presses as close to her as he can; she is wearing a woollen shawl and draws it around him so it encloses them both. He takes the end of the wool in his fingers and twirls the grey cat-softness to soothe himself. The cold

173

comes up through his legs. They should go back. He knows that. Her face has gone tight with the cold but he knows she will not move and he will not ask her to.

The house is all overgrown with briar, she says. As she knew it would be, as the girl knew it would be. And one of the walls is coming down, there are stones on the grass, it's a ruin, this little house by the edge of the sea, raised above the sand and the water that comes and goes, the sea that sees everything and says nothing but *hush, hush, hush*. She has walked all day. It's a long, slanted summer evening and the last of the sun brings out the scent of the flowers that trail in profusion here: red roses on the briar, blood red, opening their faces and hearts to the warmth of the day. Yellow keyflower, bloody crane's bill. The scent is so powerful it nearly masks the salt of the sea. Then she is lonely; then, for an instant, afraid, as the remembered scent of the white roses in her father's garden comes into her mind. But these are her father's roses too. She knows that, and feels strong. She has never left his land.

He owns the little house? the boy asks.

He was a great man, the woman says. *Almost a king, but not quite. When he stood at the top of the tallest tower of his castle, all the land he saw, in every direction, belonged to him.*

The boy, who has no place which is his own, tries to imagine this. He looks out at the sea and thinks: mine. Turns back to the land and thinks: mine. Down the path to where he knows the house is: mine. It gives him a queer feeling. He makes the word match with his heartbeat and breath: mine, mine, mine.

So as the girl comes close to the house, the woman continues, tired and hungry – she has forgotten about the remains of the bread and cheese she still carries – she stoops

174

close to one of these great red roses, its lion's face. She draws its perfume into herself and is soothed. She and the rose look at each other. It is her rose. And so she reaches into her pocket for the little golden sewing-scissors she always carries, hung from a golden chain. She neatly cuts the rose's stem.

The storyteller turns to look at the boy. She holds him tight – their noses nearly touch. Her black eyes, full of the glow of the moon, fill his vision and his heart. She looks wild, like an animal, he can feel her tremble, he is not afraid of her, he is not afraid of her, he loves her.

Just then, she says, just then the sky's brightness closed in on itself, closed down, though how the darkness came so fast the girl could hardly know. A rushing thunder-darkness all about her, holding her, from her feet to her heart to her throat. The wind came too, where there had been no wind, rising from every direction to try to throw her from where she stood, and the petals of the rose she would not relinquish yawned wide, supplicating, the stem bending, twisting. When its thorn pressed into her thumb she did not feel it.

Who are you? It was the thunder's voice, the wind's voice, ringing in her bones.

Who are you? Now she felt the thorn in her flesh. Now the flower was pulled from her grasp and petals, shrieking their red terror, fled all around, scattering.

Who are you? The thrust of the gale that forced her down on the rough ground. Now she could see nothing in the darkness that pitched around her. Her fear her blindness, her blindness her fear.

The boy looks up at the moon instead of at her savage face, listening, holding off her voice, all at once. This is her gift to him. He cannot be afraid of what she gives.

She will not release him as she speaks; tighter and tighter she holds him. She makes the girl's voice her own, the girl with the flower, the girl in the story, the woman by the house.

She said her name, the story continues in the boy's ears. She gave that wind, that force, her name. But the wind wasn't satisfied. The wind wanted more.

Why do you come here? said the wind. By what right do you come?

The boy listens to his mother's voice that rises against this wind, here, in the present, the wind that pushes against them and tries to knock them flat.

By my right, the girl said. By my own right. By what right are you here? This is my father's place. This is my father's flower. These are my father's walls. By what right do you come? Leave here, said the girl. Leave here at once.

But the spirit – for it was the spirit, the spirit of the stories she had heard, the spirit of which she had been warned, the demon she'd been told possessed this place – the spirit would not hear and would not leave.

Always the boy would remember the terror of this story, the terror of memory, the terror of the truth. Remembering what he had seen in the night between his only love and the pale-haired stranger, the stranger whose face was a mirror of his own. The stranger whose force was the wind's force, the sea's force. He had seen how she had become like the cloud, like the sand, giving way, shifting, blown and tossed in the violence of the night.

He knows this is what she is speaking of, now, when she tells the story of the spirit and the woman. What he sees in the story and what he had seen last night: they are the same. He is afraid for the girl, afraid for the girl with the flower torn from her grasp, the girl whose thumb was cut by thorn and who felt the coarse dune grass on her back as she lay helpless, understanding as little as the boy does, beneath the power of the possessing spirit, the spirit of this place. He is crying now, Tom is crying. The storyteller's voice draws back from him like the tide.

* * *

When Tom woke again he saw that she too was awake, lying in the bed, watching him. So there they were, blinking at each other. He got up, kicked the blankets back, pulled dry clothes from a box beneath the bed, dressed. It looked like a dog's nest, where he'd slept. Dust in his hair from the floor, on his cheek, but the taste of her still in his mouth.

'Do you want coffee, Janet?' he asked.

'Yes,' she said. 'I do.'

He imagined this exchange every morning. Was that every morning in the past, or every morning to come? What was the difference? There could be such simplicity in desire.

The day was fine, clear blue: but it would not last. The clouds would come over the horizon and the sky would turn white and blank, though it would not rain. Standing in the scullery he tipped coffee into the little metal pot and set it on the stove. The constant and obedient flame. He heard her get up, heard her pull the covers back up over the bed. By her footsteps he could tell where she was. There, at the old white dresser, its cracked mirror clouded with salt and age. At the cold fireplace, its men and women in their wooden shoes frozen in the daylight. By the plain table.

Condensation on the coffee pot as it warmed. He turned and stood in the scullery door.

'How's your hand?' he said. Look at all the bones of her face. She has become herself, he thought. Again in his heart this sensation, this vibration that he almost knew as joy.

'It hurts,' she said. 'It's bleeding again. There's blood on the pillow,' she said.

'That doesn't matter,' he said. He saw there was blood too on the sleeve of her clean shirt.

'The bandage came off –' she stopped. He stood looking at her. 'In the sea,' she said at last. 'With the seals. When we swam.' She nearly laughed, and bit her lip. The coffee pot began to hiss, and he turned back and took it off the stove. 'I don't have milk,' he said. 'It will have to be black.'

'Fine,' she said. Her voice even.

'Here,' he said, 'let me do this first.' Quickly and neatly he wrapped her hand again; how different it was now that their bodies were accustomed to moving against each other, even in these small, useful movements their bodies understood each other, he thought.

Then he poured the coffee, oily and dark; set two mugs on the table and they sat. As they had sat the night before; but not as they had sat the night before. The night before, before – before damage, before restitution, though he would not have been able to say which was which, or what they sat in the midst of now.

Then she said: 'I can't –' She leaned her forehead into her good hand. He wanted to touch her. He did not. 'Who are you?'

'I told you,' he said. 'My name is Tom.'

Now she laughed, her head thrown back. Her white throat. A mark on it, a mark he'd made.

'And my name is Janet,' she said. 'We've done that already. We've done a lot more. Last night . . . This was an empty house.'

'No,' he said, as gently as he could.

'I couldn't throw you out,' she said. 'Stupid – to think I

178

could.' She was staring at him. 'This was my mother's place. This is my mother's place. My mother –'

'You don't know who she was.'

'No,' she said. 'No I don't. And I'm afraid to ask, why do you know that? But I guess I shouldn't be afraid of anything after last night. After –'

'What happened to you?'

'Nothing,' she said. 'In the morning, almost morning, you mean. A seizure. Something in my brain, it's just – I don't know. It's hard to explain. It's just electricity, it's just neurons, or whatever they are.' Her face was earnest. 'But it takes me to another place. It feels like this place, now. Maybe that doesn't make any sense,' Janet said. Her eyes on him were clear and true. She was trying to give him something, despite herself. 'But that's not what I mean. Except I wasn't surprised, by that. I wasn't surprised by anything. And I don't know how that's possible. Here with you. Tom. Tom with his whisky and fucking, here at the end of the world.'

'You came to the end of the world,' he said. 'You're right. It is the end of the world. That's why I came here. That's why she brought me here.'

He saw how it stopped her: *she*.

'Who?'

The coffee was no longer steaming; had already begun to cool. Neither of them had drunk. He would rather have had more whisky, but he did not move for the bottle.

'You could have stopped me.'

'You're changing the subject.'

'No,' he said. 'I'm not.'

'Yes,' she said. 'I could have stopped you. But I suppose if I wanted to stop you I wouldn't have followed you into this house. This house. Listen to me. My house. My bed.

You came into my bed.'

'Our bed?'

'I don't think so.' He saw she meant it. 'Now listen to me. Who. You tell me who. Who brought you here? Tom. Do you have a last name, Tom?'

'Do you?'

'I am asking you questions. You are not asking me. You have had enough. You have had enough.'

'Enough of you? I don't think so.'

It was true as he said it, as he held her gaze in this whitening morning and the thought of building a fire went from him because he felt the fire in himself. He held her wrist on the table and moved again towards her, his hand on the back of her skull to hold her, to feel her opening mouth, her tongue, her teeth, and then her palm flat on his chest, shoving him away, hard with the strength of her rage. The slap landed flat on his cheek, her knuckle on the bone below his eye, and the pain was like a blast of cold air on him, waking him, bringing him to life. The light in her eyes.

'No,' he said. 'I don't think so.'

She pushed back from the table, the chair tipping back behind her, falling. She moved to the fireplace, crouched down, looking at nothing, at the grate. Then at the tiles.

'Look at them,' she said finally. 'The little blue people. Watching us.'

'That's what I used to think,' he said. 'I could never remember which tile was which. I thought they moved around. Had adventures. The people in the tiles.'

'I'm sorry I hit you,' she said.

'No,' he said. 'You're not.'

It was then she started to cry. He didn't move. There was no comfort here. He had never found comfort here. He wouldn't offer her a lie.

'Sometimes,' he said, 'I thought she might tell me stories about the people in the tiles, those blue people. With their wooden shoes. But she never did. They don't matter, the stories in the tiles. If there are any. They're not our stories. They just happen to be here. Some things here are important. Some things aren't. You have to learn to tell the difference. If you're looking for answers, you won't find them. I stopped looking. It's better that way.'

She lifted up her shirt to wipe at her eyes; he saw the white stripe of her belly. She shivered. She got up, pulled another sweater from her bag, dragged it awkwardly over her head.

'I'll lay a fire,' he said.

'I'd decided I could live without them,' she said at last. She drank her cooling coffee. 'Answers. Years ago. I didn't need them, there was enough. My father – it was enough. I didn't want to ask him what he didn't want to tell me. We were just – complete. I didn't need anything else.'

He listened, moving by the fireplace where there was wood neatly stacked, kindling, some paper. Her father. A quick crushing in his chest when he saw her in his mind's eye, as a little girl, walking somewhere in the world as he had walked, not knowing she was lost, deciding with the certainty of childhood that it was all complete. So he had decided. So children decide. Then they discover otherwise.

'Please tell me,' she said. 'Please.' A sound like something had gone out of her. The fire came to life. A thread of smoke after the match, the splinters of kindling glowing red, black, curling in on themselves.

'Come here,' he said. 'Come close, here. Keep warm.' There was nothing to sit on, before the fire; he took the blankets that had been his bed and folded them in front of the hearth. She came, and she sat, and he sat down too, so they were side by side. A hair's breadth between their shoulders and in him again was the memory of this sensation, this proximity. He turned his head to see her profile set against the stone wall, the little window; the fire had brought spots of colour to her cheeks and her hair straggled down out of its plait. She had drawn her legs up, wrapped her arms around them; then she rested her cheek on her knee and looked at him. He was trembling and wondered if she could feel it. She must. His violence and hers, and now what seemed to be tenderness. He let it rise for a moment like the fire rose, strengthening, taking.

Then he got up from his place before the fire and walked to the old white dresser. The drawers stuck on themselves; he rarely opened them. He tried the first drawer, and then the second. He never remembered which drawer they were in; he had decided this must be on purpose, how he erased this recollection. There was not much choice. There were not many important objects in this place. Still, he had to hunt for her. She did not come easily to his hand.

There. The second drawer. He pushed them both closed, hearing the complaint of the wood, the soft click of the little metal handles as they swung against themselves. It was such a gentle sound. It was a sound that belonged in a comfortable bedroom with wallpaper and calico curtains, not a sound for this place. He returned to where she sat, the two photographs in his hand.

He gave them to her. She sat with her knees up, her newly bandaged hand held stiff, but with its fingers she fanned the two images like cards. She leaned slightly forward. Then she was still, very still, as she stared at them in the pallid light.

The first of a smiling woman. Her face. Her dark hair, in a plait, running down over her shoulders. Her dark eyes.

The photograph was black and white – and browning at its edges – but there was no mistaking the colour of her hair and eyes. They sucked the light in, away from the whiteness of her skin that was stretched taut over her fine bones, the arches of her brow, the cut-curve of her lip, her nose not quite symmetrical, not quite beautiful, but in the eyes that gazed down out of the present and into the past, perfect, perfect, perfect.

He couldn't hear her breathe. She was holding her breath. Looking at the woman. The photograph. The mirror. He remembered how it was when he'd seen the spirit of this place, his father, when he was a boy. The mirror of himself. He saw that in Janet now.

The next photograph: the same woman, at a distance. By a house in a city somewhere, wearing a skirt that would have been, then, too long to be fashionable and a rollneck sweater drawn up against her chin. She leaned against the bricks behind her; right at the edge of the image there was a street sign but it gave away nothing. High, it said, the rest must have been High Street, he'd long thought that, but he didn't remember it. Who had taken the photograph? When was it? He had no idea. Now it was in her hands, in Janet's hands, so it must exist. Sometimes he had disbelieved its existence. The proof of her, here.

She was not alone in this photograph. There he was, looking up at her, this little boy, his face blurred in turning towards her as the shutter clicked but his white hair in a cloud around his face unmistakable. They were holding hands, the black-haired woman and the white-haired boy. Lost in the past, locked together, the black-haired woman, the white-haired boy.

'You see,' he said. 'Your mother. You look like her. You see?'

He was standing behind her. Something had rolled in the dressing-table drawer when he'd opened it, rolled forward from the back with a sound like a pinball headed down a chute. It was not often he let himself lift this out, open the little tube, twist up the stick of bright red wax. The name of the colour was printed in dim gold at the bottom; the case was made to look as if it were twined with vines, with leaves. She had not seen; nor even, perhaps, heard. He let his nostrils catch the scent of the stuff, faded and sticky; then he set it back where it had been. 'Your mother,' he said. 'And mine.'

CHAPTER ELEVEN

They were so ordinary, the photographs.

They were objects.

There were so many objects in the world. Her car, this book, that table, these photographs. What they had in common was their separateness, that they could be touched but never taken in, there was no need to absorb them, no possibility of absorption. The torn photographs she'd found that time. Found and put away from herself, from her mind, and now sitting in front of his fire she saw herself again barefoot, running and running, with those torn photographs in her hand although she had never held them again. In this vision she was running and she was standing still. She was two women. Who was this woman in front of the fire, with these photographs in her hand?

The woman in the photographs. Her mother. How the body does not lie. Looking at the photographs like looking into a glass.

Janet could still feel the wetness between her legs. His wetness and hers. She had not washed.

She could throw the images into the fire. Then they would never have been. Then nothing would exist. It was like the temptation, when standing on some high place, to jump. She knew she would not. Carefully she set them down beside her, just to her right, one overlapping the other as if they were playing cards. Then she turned her head away, rested her cheek on her knees. He still stood. Tom. She could see his shins, his ankles, his feet – he was dressed, of course, now, as she was; but she recalled the sensation of his bone against the flesh of her calf, her heel kicking against his in that bed, that bed over there.

'I don't remember where they were taken,' he said, finally. 'I don't know who took them. You think I'd remember something like that, someone must have given them to her. We didn't have a camera or anything. Ever. She didn't care about those things. It's queer how people go through life, don't you think, always taking pictures, insisting on souvenirs, like they have to prove they exist. Look, I can show you, here, I'm real. But there they are. I guess I'm glad I have them, now.'

'Were they here in this house? When you came here?'

'No,' he said. 'I had them with me. I don't keep much. But I kept these. I don't really know why. Well, yes I do. Like I said. Proof.'

She was listening to him speaking as if she would listen to anyone else. She felt hollowed out. He sat down again, close to her, and she was glad of it, his presence, his solid shape, there, against her shoulder. Not desire. Desire was not the name for this. But it behaved as desire behaved, scooping at her gut and making her skin prickle, raising the down on her arm, on the back of her neck. She did not look at him but let her eyes get hot from holding them wide at the fire which devoured itself, which demanded more, which cracked and spat from scarlet, to gold, to fierce, empty white.

'I was a boy when we came here,' he said. 'It was after that. After these pictures, whenever they were. I was older. Not much, but older than that.'

She adjusted the pictures at her side, for something to do. 'I guess that's you,' she said. Janet reached up and ran her bandaged hand over his strawy head. Left a track.

She was looking into his eyes. She wanted to look into his eyes, they were the same as the fire. She stared and couldn't stop staring. 'Look,' she said, glancing down at her clotted bandages. Blood had begun to seep through again. 'It hurts.'

When he had worked on her it felt like a ritual. Like something he had always done and would always do. They had stood side by side at the stone sink as he unwrapped her and ran freezing water from the tap over the cut until it all ran clear into the drain. She could imagine standing here when she was an old woman and he was an old man, bent and shrivelled, still tending her unhealed wound. Tending his, too: the only difference was that his, you could not see. Her heart, her hand, her whole body. She could have tried to push him away. He was what she was, herself. That, she could not push away.

Metal in her mouth.

'Christ,' she said, and held his arm. Why was there only weakness here? She had come for strength.

'What?'

'The same as before. As when –'

'When you came?'

Christ, Christ. 'Yes,' she said. 'Yes. Leave me alone. Don't go, don't.'

'Which is it?'

'Don't go.' And he held her again, in front of the streaky glass with the sea outside, the rough wall of gorse outside, the wild garlic on the path outside, it was all outside and she was here, tight against him. She held him hard, and the sucked shell of her rage splintered against his ribs. The sea receding, the seizure receding, leaving her flat and blank as wet sand.

He let go. They both did.

'What is it like?' he asked.

'I can't tell you more than I did. Like another place. I used to have them when I was a little girl. They went away. Now they've come back. Not too long ago, they came back.'

'It frightens you.'

'I don't know,' she said. 'Yes. It shouldn't, they shouldn't. I know what they are. I think it's because of where they happen. Happen in my brain, I mean. It's like – like leaving. Not for anywhere pleasant. But then it goes, so – it doesn't matter.'

Close by her now, he put two more dry branches on the licking flame. She could see that the day, which had begun blue, was beginning to close over, the sky whitening. She had been here – how long? Only hours, hours. Stephen would be . . . she could not imagine. How she had used to think of his day, her day, separate and united, glancing at the clock in the centre and knowing that he would be arriving in a studio, or at a theatre, or a school, or sitting in their kitchen or crossing the street. She recalled the noise of her mobile cracking under her boot heel. That was not the reason he was lost to her, now.

Strange, how clean the realisation was, on this ordinary morning where everything was changed. Standing in the cold, in the black night, by the sea: the word in her head, the word for what she sought. It could not have been *mother*. She had allowed him to take her: and he knew. Not mother. Brother. And now there was no going back. It was simple, obvious. If it was awful – what was the point of thinking that? Awful. *Aweful*.

188

She tried to bring Stephen's face into her mind. Nothing came. Was it her choice, or had he turned his back to her? It did not matter. He was gone. That was the only truth there was.

There were the photographs, where she'd left them.

'My father,' she said. 'My father said she died. My mother. I was three years old. She went out, one evening, just around the corner from our house, just to buy something, just an ordinary evening, and a drunk driver jumped the kerb and killed her. Like that. In an instant. People say, people said when I was older, of course they didn't say then, at least she didn't suffer. I don't remember her. My father –'

Again they sat side by side. Hidden from everything and everyone, in this stone shelter. She could have believed that with her brass key she had called it into existence, summoned it, that it had not existed before her arrival – except there had been the ash in the grate, the whisky and the broken glass, Tom, his pale head and dark eyes. They were nothing alike. But the taste of him had been the taste of herself. That she had known all along.

'My father loved her so much he wouldn't talk about that, about the end. He said I was enough for him, I was her daughter, she was still there, with us. In me. Not that we were the same, but – well, that's what he said.' She was not speaking to Tom, although Tom was listening. 'I never thought that before. Whatever you grow up with: that's how it is. That's normal.'

When she picked up the photographs again the deckled edges vibrated, as if they would call a note out of the air, the music of the past.

'I don't know what she looks like. I mean: I didn't know what she looked like. Everyone I knew had photographs, pictures on the bookshelves or in albums, Christmas cards

– we didn't. I never thought it was strange or anything. Like you said. No pictures, just life, going on, not stuck into pictures you could keep, that showed you how happy you were. People never have pictures of themselves when they're sad, I don't think. The pictures are only to show you how happy you are.' Then she said: 'How old are you?'

He told her. Four years between them. Four years, an ocean, another life.

* * *

It is a summer night and he is sitting at the edge of my bed. Sometimes he smooths the covers, tucked over me, or loops my hair back behind my ear. This story of how they met: why do I want to hear it, over and over again? I like beginnings. I am not interested in endings. I think I know something about endings, that they are unlikely to be good. I like potential, the power that's there at the start, before entropy kicks in.

She'd lost her key, he says. Standing on the frozen steps in a short wool coat and heavy black shoes. I remember her shoes. My father is not looking at me, he is looking out of the window, as if he can see her there, just beyond the glass, walking in the air. They were like men's shoes, he says, the best she could do against the cold.

Blast, she was saying, and the air was so still her voice carried in the dark. Everything was hushed up with the cold and her voice seemed loud. She didn't even have a hat. Her hair was very dark, like yours. She had black wool gloves and she put a black hand on her forehead. Her white forehead.

There were six steps to her door. Funny what you remember, isn't it? Like the shoes. I counted when I went up. One, two, three, four, five, six: Can I help? Or something like that, I must have said. See, I remember the steps, but not exactly what I said to her. To your mother. Funny.

She lived in a little flat on the first floor, which is what they call it there, we'd call it the second floor, but I was just learning all that then. (Lying there in my pyjamas, looking up at him, I try to store this away, some fragment of truth about her. It is a solid piece of information that I could feed into myself and – what? Become her? If, like her, I would say the first floor when I meant the second?)

We went and had a drink. There was a pub around the corner, a bar, it was called The Engineer. She was shivering, her gloves were no good and underneath them her fingers looked like twigs, white, stripped of bark, pink at the tips. I got two glasses of whisky because if you're cold, whisky is the drink, and when I sat down across from her, her hands were on the wooden table with its coloured beer mats and I picked them up in my two hands and blew on them, to warm her.

Of course he takes my hands in his to show me, even though it is summer, even though it is hot, too hot. My hands outside the covers now, cupping my fingers in his own and blowing, puff, puff, puff. It tickles. It makes me laugh.

See? he says. Just like that. She laughed.

How old am I, at this telling? A little older. When I was younger he would just tell me the story. He wouldn't tell me how he felt. Now he says: she was so beautiful. Her head right back, laughing. I'd never seen anyone so beautiful. Well, he says, looking down at me, smiling, until I saw you. My little girl. Not so little. I'm so proud of you.

For what? I must have said.

Just for being you. We have to love each other, he says,

for what we are. Not for what we want to be, or what we want other people to be. They can't be any different. Not in their true hearts.

Silence, a little.

The whisky revived us, he says, and maybe she forgot I'd held her hands but I didn't forget. She told me her name was Margaret, that she worked in a bookshop, and I could tell from her voice that she didn't come from where we were but I didn't know enough to be able to hear where it was she came from. She told me she had a downstairs neighbour, the neighbour on the ground floor, we'd say the first floor, who had a key to her flat too but the neighbour was away.

I asked her if she had a friend she could call. Yes, she said, I do, and so when we'd finished our drinks I walked her to a telephone booth, a call box, and I don't know why, I'm sure she had money, but I gave her change to make a phone call and stood outside the metal and glass door while she dialled, while she dropped the coins into the slot. She hadn't even bothered to put her gloves back on, they were useless, her wrists were so white in the darkness, the cord from the telephone curling down by her ear. She was smiling at me through the glass, my father says to me, and I was standing close to the glass so my breath made fog on it, melted the ice crystals that formed and re-formed in the freezing night. It was night now, or nearly. Nearly.

And it's night now, here, for me in my bed. I want him to go on. I don't say anything because if I do he'll realise it's late, that he should tell me goodnight, let me read for a little while on my own. I listen to records, too, before I go to sleep. I have a record player that holds up a stack of three flat black vinyl discs, and if I am falling asleep the pause, click, drop of the next record will pull me back into wakefulness, just a little. The records are ready to go. Kids' songs, I listen to, only there's one record I like too, my father's, I wish I still had it: the sound of a double bass that makes me think of the ocean, or a cave, somewhere deep and safe.

She said, No one's home, when she came out of the phone box. She rubbed her hands together, rubbed her own red cheeks, standing there.

(Later I will wonder if this is true. Only later, much later. What if she never called anyone? What if she had made another choice, there, in the pub, out of the cold, with my father, a stranger, another choice for another life? Right there, right then. In an instant everything can change.)

So, my father then says, almost lightly, as if it is nothing, so, I said, well, why don't you come home with me? Just for a little while. Then you can call your friends again. I told her I had some soup, or something, some bread and cheese, we could eat that and then she could go out to the call box outside and try again. I didn't have a telephone of my own. Almost no one did, even people who weren't renting rooms like I was.

I remember, my father says, how asking her back to my room was the first thing that made me feel like I belonged in this place, in this city, even though I knew I didn't. Normally, when you come to a strange place, people help you, that's how it is, and usually for quite a long while. Like when Miss Marshall moved into the upstairs apartment a couple of years ago. You even took her out to the deli once, didn't you? Well, you went out together, I knew you'd be safe with her, but you showed her the way. Now she knows the way. But I suppose she was helping you too, that time, taking you out.

Listen to my father, talking to himself, not really talking

193

to me, I am the vessel he pours himself into, he holds his memories by tipping them into me. But he believes I am a small cup. He will only pour so much. He worries I will spill.

It was good to be able to help her, Margaret. Margaret who had lost her key. So that was how we met, you know that, your mother and I. That was how we met. It was so cold. She couldn't get into her house. I took her to my place. You know, my father says, I didn't have any soup. It didn't seem to matter.

Night slipping in through the blinds. The hiss of the turntable, the music's caress in my solitary sleep, so warm, so happy, alone in my narrow bed. Dreaming of two sets of footsteps, side by side on an icy pavement, walking forward into the future. My future.

* * *

Why should it be different because of what she knows, knows now? That he is not a stranger. That he is her blood. That he must have known it as soon as he saw her face, her hands, her skin. Her feet when he unlaced her boots.

She had never tried to imagine what it would be like to have a brother or a sister. To be *only* was so much a part of her; it would have been like trying to imagine another limb. Why would you?

Could she have known the truth, too? Could she have prevented it? Why had she allowed him – not just him, any-one – to act as he had done? Something had happened to her here that was a force beyond her control. The force of her desire to find something, no matter what it was. Or per-haps, not quite awake to the figure who'd stood over her bed, she had been dreaming of Stephen. Had believed the present might be the past, the always irrecoverable past. Stephen. She had known it was gone, that easy past, as soon as she had stepped over the threshold of this door, the door she had called her own though it was not in her possession, though there had been fire in the abandoned grate and this white-haired spirit here in haunting.

Who was a spirit? Who was not? She had seen on the mantelpiece a mask, a mask made of rusted iron with a brazen mouth and the open slashes of its eyes where the metal had been heated, torn, staved in by accident or design, she could not tell. An abstract face, a woman's face. It was the only object of decoration in this, her half-derelict, stolen inheritance. She had looked into its face and looked away. She had not wished to recognise it.

If she had been dreaming of that mask, that face, it was a dream so buried she could not retrieve it. Her injury, the whisky, her exhaustion had made her plunge into sleep as soon as she had lain flat under the thin covers; Janet was lucky. In the worst of times she had always been able to vanish into her cave of sleep. She was a diver with oxygen, a man on the moon. She was beyond anyone's reach. But her dreams came; and perhaps this one had been of Stephen. Sometimes the fantastical visions of her nights let her alone, and she was allowed something closer to simplicity or memory. She had let herself fall, this night, into the wedding that had tempted her for an instant – among the candles and among the guests – towards that whiteness, that daytime dream of a new beginning. The daytime dream that had made her mind close on itself, fire on itself, make its own world of sparks and shocks in order to effect an escape. Walking home beside him, in her dream her uninjured palm close against his, their fingers twined in a lovers' knot of flesh. But her vision did not end in unity: in her dream, then, there came an unlacing towards solitude. Walking away through the yellow night city, the pavement rough against the bare soles of her feet. And as she walked the blood flowing away from her, from between her thighs, swirling down into water, into the city's dark river.

Her father had never been strict with her when she was a girl. It had been the two of them, they were a team. They made the rules they needed, though you could not have called them rules. *I trust your judgment*, he'd say, even when she was quite small. He was right to trust that judgment. Aware that something had been taken from her, something she could never replace, she kept herself within certain boundaries, as if to transgress would be to reopen the door through which fragility entered, through which loss had slipped through. She was very careful crossing the street.

Yet she had been aware that she could have asked for anything.

She had kept silent.

She thought of a time, years in the future, when those boundaries would blur, or vanish. She would feel safer. Then she could make any choice.

This choice.

Would he have stopped? If she had said: *do not*. The choice, too, to keep silent, to lie still and look up in the half-dark and find him standing there, his eyes hidden in their sockets but their black light pouring down on her all the same.

When she was a little girl she had wondered, so many times, what would happen if you –

If you –

If you crossed the bridge alone, if you let go of your father's hand.

Tom held her down as if she would have fought or as if she were fighting, his grip on her so the blood came again to her palm. The pain reminded her of who she was, of her choice. She was shaking. She could feel her bones, her muscles, sinews, veins and arteries, moving against each other, her awareness of her own body the understanding that kept her from flying apart. When he opened her mouth with his own mouth she had tried to recall Stephen's but that was gone, that was another life, there was no possibility of retrieval.

His hands at her clothes, pulling and tearing, this struggle in the dark that was clear as time. She put her lips on the flesh of his neck, her teeth scraping on his collarbone, and even this close, how queer, but impossible to catch his scent. There was nothing. The iron of her blood, her own sweat, her own sex – but from him a clean emptiness, only sensation. As if all her other senses had been cancelled by touch. It flayed her, what she wanted, what she had to have.

The old sheet against her nipples now, her shirt pulled up, his breath in her ear and her other life, the past suddenly whole before her. This was a mistake, but it was too late, her legs were open, his whole weight on her and she felt that strange, familiar smoothness – anyone's prick, it could have been, but it was this one now, fitting as the moment did, isolated, pure. She closed her eyes, her arms stretched right above her. Details she would recall. Her good hand on the chipped enamel of the bedstead, how cold it was in her curled fingers. Her jeans crumpled on the stone-flagged floor: as he pushed himself into her she saw herself in the six a.m. light of her own bedroom, pulling them on, fastening the buttons, buckling her belt, sitting back down on the edge of the bed to draw on the pair of thick green wool socks she still wore, her toes flexing inside them as she shifted her weight under his, the bones of her hips pressing into the thin mattress. Feeling the suck from the cup of air opening up between the curve of his belly and the curve of her back. He bit at her ear, her left ear, a flare of heat from his teeth and his tongue. His breath and the sound of the breathing sea drew in and out together. Somewhere the pair of seals was diving, catching silver fish in their sharp teeth, breaking the surface of the water to turn their abyssal eyes to the land.

* * *

Here is where my father will talk about the next beginning, the new-found land. It is autumn, I am sure it is, the air is polished, shining with first cold. We are walking through a little park, hardly a park, a plaza, the leaves of the scraggly trees hanging on the branches as they turn and curl, baring their ribs, before winter. We are holding hands, swinging our arms, we are laughing as the path turns down on to a sidewalk and then down again into the shadow under the bridge. You can miss the steps if you don't know they're there, but I know, I can't imagine not knowing this and one day I am shocked when a stranger asks us, How do I get to the bridge? Even though we are standing right there. Here it is, my father says. Hey!

Up the stone steps which lead to the wooden walkway. Rising, rising, we are walking in step, it must be a Sunday morning and we are going to have dim sum over the river, which is something we like to do. We never ask what's on the little carts, my dad never does, he just says, Yes, one of those. Let's eat till we can't see, he'll say, and I still think this is funny. I don't know why.

The wooden walkway that arches out over the river, this

beautiful, eternal invitation. The walkway rises as the cables of the bridge rise in what my father has taught me is called a catenary curve, the perfect curve that is itself: how a cord would hang if you held its ends between your index finger and thumb. Wire laid against wire, wire coiled on wire, wire crossed with wire, and stone, limestone and granite, shouldering up out of the deep river's bed. Cyclists stand on their pedals to surmount the ascent to the centre; the ones coming the other way, towards us, coast and float downhill until they brake, swing their legs over saddles, hoist their bikes on their shoulders and carry them down the stairs. Someone, a woman in an orange scarf and no hat, her blonde hair pushed back by the quick breeze, sits on a bench with a cup of coffee, looking as if in another moment it's going to be too cold to sit here, to sit still, but she doesn't want to leave yet. Not yet. We walk by her. My father is speaking. His voice sings in me and in the wires of the bridge. The city's bay opens up, south of us, lapped with the possibility of the sea.

I brought her here, he says. The very first morning after we arrived. Another voyage across the ocean he'd made, only this time not alone, this time there was a groom and his bride, a man and his wife, to work away at the five thousand pieces of the jigsaw puzzle (it was the same ship; it was the same puzzle; not much progress had been made) and swirl glasses of brandy as they sat in two deckchairs under the round bold eye of a violet moon. I worried she would be seasick, he says, but she never was, even though the first two days it was so rough you had to walk, or try to walk, with your legs wide apart as if you were trying to straddle the whole ship, and stick close to the walls where there were rails to hang on to. In the dining room there were clips to hold the plates to the tables. The first night, in a bucket clamped to a table, there was a bottle of champagne for us from the captain.

The real captain of the ship? I used to ask. A mythical figure with a white beard and a pipe, standing at a great spoked wheel and keeping a weather eye out for pirates.

The real captain of the ship, he'd say, in those days. A bottle of champagne, because we were newlyweds. We finished it, in our cabin. We didn't even have a window. Only two bunk beds. Sitting on the bottom bunk, we drank it all. We got a little drunk. Your mother. Your mother and I.

We are not quite at the middle of the bridge. A stone tower ahead of us, invincible. How I love this place that is no place, that is a step over the void, that holds me steady and is never still.

My father says: two lovers can sleep on the blade of a knife. And then he blushes. We don't speak for a little while. One bicycle. Two the other way. Look up. Below a hollow cut in the stone high above, chalky streaks trail down the granite face, and there is the neat Horus head of the falcon who roosts there. I point, and my father tips his head back and just as he does the bird opens its wings and drops down into the air, catching the wind, dipping through the wires and away over the city.

When we got here, my father says, everything was new. To her, I mean, he says – but what that meant was, it was new to me too. Everything. How she would stand on the steps of a bus with her palm out flat, trying to remember what each silver coin was worth, which ones had ridged edges, which ones were smooth. She hated the milk. The milk was all wrong. (How could that be? Milk was milk. Of all the drinks in the world, how could there be any alteration, any difference, in milk?) Mostly, of course, she didn't hate things, I don't mean to sound – well, she wasn't like that, but when you are away from home you miss familiar things. Even if you've wanted to get away. I suppose what you discover is –

Now we are standing together, looking towards the bottom of the city, the island, the tidal strait that pours and shudders between, under, the trusswork, the towers, another arch of steel suspended in the hazed distance, the raised torch unlit behind the ordinary orange of a passing ferry boat. If I close my eyes I will see this too, I know it so well, it's imprinted in me, my father has put it there, I have put it there myself. It is ours. It anchors me. Sometimes, when the seizures come, it is this view I'll try to capture, to recall, to bring me back. It never works. It stays separate. It is insulated, safe, unshocked by the electrics of my mind.

The cable sweeps up over our heads, shifting in its steel saddle, in tension, alive. The force in the wire I can feel in the steel beam against my belly, in the wood under my feet. My empty belly; I begin to think about dumplings and pork, the salty glaze of hoisin sauce. For a moment I'm not listening. Just for a moment.

I suppose what you discover is that you can't get away, my father says. There's always something to miss. Even the things you hate. Even the things you fear. They are just inside you, right next to the things you love, twisted together with the things you love. He is not looking at the thin cables that drop vertically, diagonally, from the main cables to the bridge floor, but I am, and I see how they are twisted together, fused so they could never be unsealed. The things you love, the things you hate.

It's not true, what I said before. Sometimes I hate that I have no mother, yes, I want to know; but I love my father. I love that he is mine, that we are ours, that there is no one between us. Twisted like steel cable, hate and love, love and hate.

You can't get away, he says. What makes you what you are, holds you. He holds me now, his arm tight around me. You can't escape. It will pull you back and you'll have no choice.

Look how the sunlight glows in his eyes, makes them shine, as if with tears.

* * *

A while later, Janet and Tom walked out through the green door, back along the coastal path towards where the seals had been, and where they had been with the seals. It seemed long ago now, as if these hours had been their whole lives. The sky was sheeted as candlewax now, alabaster, high, a lid of cloud closed over them. She was waiting to hear him speak.

'The track you came along,' he said. 'The brambles there. We picked blackberries, the first time I came. I thought that's all we'd have to eat, blackberries. It was just this time of year.'

She wondered how old he had been then. She knew how old he was now. She put the calculation away, held it at a distance from her, what it meant. She didn't ask him the question.

'I was just a boy,' he said, almost as if he had heard her, 'little, not so little . . . I'm not sure. I didn't know much, that makes you little. I just followed her. I followed her everywhere. Of course I did. But she went, is what I mean. Left one place and then another, as if she wasn't at home anywhere. She left and left. We did, I mean. We were always leaving. She was never settled. She would get a job somewhere – I think – make money, somehow, and I would go to school, wherever it was, a town or a city, usually, and I wouldn't know anyone and I wouldn't know anything, and then we would leave again. I didn't care much, I think. I was with her. It was all right. I would make things. I was good with my hands.'

'That mask,' she said. 'Or whatever it is. Face. That doesn't belong in the house.'

'It does,' he said. The push of his voice. 'I made it. That's what I do.'

'You're a – a sculptor?'

The darkness that crossed his face. 'No,' he said. 'I fix cars. I work in a garage here. That's how I live. You wouldn't be imagining I was anything special, now, would you?'

His face was as pale as the sky, as unreadable. 'No,' she said quickly. 'Don't worry.'

'I won't,' he said.

The cord between them, first tight, then slack. Wound in her grasp, around her spine, around her heart.

'She would – I don't know. All my life, my young life, when we were together she would – tell me stories. Awful stories, I guess you'd say, if you heard them, they weren't stories for a child. Demons and spirits and – suffering. Or something.' His laugh was a harsh bark in the air. 'I guess you'd say they were about love, if you could call it that. It gave me – maybe it gave me the wrong idea.' Did he look at her sidelong? A flicker in the corner of her eye, the possibility of his glance.

'Are you telling me you're sorry?' She made her voice cold.

'No,' he said. 'I'm not. I'm telling you what happened.'

She was quiet, let him be.

'The things I make. Sometimes I think they're like those

203

stories, though I don't even know what that means. Like I could make them solid.'

'Like you could get her back?'

'Yes,' he said.

In that moment she loved him. They wanted the same thing. They were the same thing. She could never forgive him, but she loved him. What love or forgiveness was – they were only words. But the openness in her heart was real.

'Anyway, never mind what I make. Then we came here. It was different here. She knew this place. This house, it didn't frighten her the way it frightened me. She said it was home. She'd never said that about anywhere, she didn't believe in that, it never existed. And the place she wanted for home – I was scared to death of it.'

'I can't imagine you scared.' An allowance made.

He looked at her then, but not at her, she thought, within himself, his gaze rocking back in towards that boy by the sea so long ago.

'I was,' he said. 'What we found here – what she found –'

The wind skipped up off the water, flung itself in their faces, slapped at their coats. How queer it had been to walk past her car, parked so tidily there by the house, and at any time she could have unlocked its door, turned the key in the ignition, driven away, down and down, back to pavements, streetlamps, warm life. But the other key, the key to her mother's house, seemed to cancel out the other, like magnets held so they repel.

'What was it?' she asked. 'What did she find?'

'I think you find what you want, here. That seems to be the way. Don't you think?'

The rocks stubbed up sharp beneath her feet, shoved through the earth of the path, wouldn't be hidden, and the gorse was a yellow violence on the dunes. The sea pulled back from the shore so that it too was revealed, tangled wracks of stinking kelp, mussels yawning open, dead, a plastic bottle, a huddle of frayed polymer rope. Wreckage thrown up from the water, from where the black-eyed seals hid. Once you were here there was nowhere else to run. Here was the end of the hunt.

'My father was here,' he said after a while. 'At least, well, he must have been, my father, the man we met. She never said in so many words. But it seemed she must have left him, and come back. He looked like me. Just like me.' He turned to face her. He stood too close. She wished he would stand closer. How did she become this, this creature of want and dread? Her hair, loosed from its plait, was gripped by the wind, loosed, gripped again, as she herself was loosed and gripped by whatever need had drawn her, the longing she'd pinned back for so long, tied into a knot whose heart was hidden even from her own soul's gaze. All her father's stories of beginnings, the beautiful beginnings, a new world, a new love. Here she stood at the end of things, at the edge. *I dreamt I went to my mother's grave.* The wind that had blown through her in that dream as her beautiful mother, the woman with her own face, her own bones, her own translucent skin, had sat propped against the greening stone in her blanket of earth, waiting, waiting.

Waiting for this. Closer, come closer, she didn't say to him, but he did come closer until they stood breast to breast on the path.

Waiting for you, he'd said.

She remembered once, when she had been six or seven, she had decided one afternoon just to look out of her bedroom window, look down the street, towards the corner. She had watched the lights change, over and over, red to green, green to red. She had seen taxi-cabs swish by and women with strollers and a boy who left a box on the sidewalk and kept walking. It felt like she sat there for hours and hours, watching. She jumped when she heard her father's voice. What are you doing? he asked. Looking for Mom, she said. She was shocked herself, how clear it was in her now, at the words she made with her own mouth, but her father – he sat down, so fast it was as if someone had knocked the backs of his knees with a broom, bump on the edge of her bed. He looked at her, his child, for a long time. Then he got up, turned, and simply left the room.

She had lost that memory until now.

Waiting for you. Closer, come closer.

'You knew what you were to me,' she said. 'You knew.'

'Yes,' he said again. His confirmation of her. 'I don't have any excuse.'

'No,' she answered. 'But then – neither do I.'

CHAPTER TWELVE

To the north the broken jaw of the ruined castle lay shattered on the cliff, a couple of miles away; the stones just a darker shade than the sky, charcoal. The same colour as the stone of the house, The Shieling, waiting patiently behind them as, he thought, it had always waited. Perhaps his fear of this place, when he was a child, had come from his desire to imagine some separation between himself and it. Once, he'd had some hope that he had no connection to the stories mortared into the fabric of the building, stories not spoken but inhabited as a house is inhabited, a home. No place like home. You can't go home again.

But there was only home. Standing on the shore with her, describing in fragments the stories he'd heard of longing and blood. He had never meant them to come alive, but then he had never meant anything to happen at all. Even after his mother had left him he was still, somehow, following where she led, listening to her, believing her. He had had no other choice. Now, just now, he was glad. Janet had described to him the storms in her head, the seizures; he'd seen them. They too were familiar, part of him. Seized.

He had never tried to imagine another life for himself. The years of drifting had been what he'd always known, an echo of the life he'd lived with her, a hope that in the echo he could hear love spoken, feel warmth against his heart.

But there had been no such thing. There was no such thing. It was a trick, a vanishing act, a strand of black hair across white wool, only relic or illusion: there was no way to tell.

'The stories she told me,' he said. 'They weren't – Cinderella, is that what you tell kids? They were harder than that. Metal, like I said.'

He saw in Janet's face that she pictured him, the straw-headed boy, listening to stories. In her eyes there was a look of appetite, greed, not so different from what had risen up in her under his hands, his hands on her flesh.

'When I was older I asked how she knew them all. There were so many. She just – laughed. It was like she didn't understand the question. How could you not know them? I just do, she said, or something like that. Stories are stories. They're true, so you know them. Everyone knows what's true.'

'Do they?' Her voice sparked against him like a struck flint.

'Do they what?'

'Know what's true. Do they know what's true?' It was almost scorn in her voice. 'I didn't. I thought something else was true. I thought my mother was dead and my father loved me. My father told me stories, you know. About – himself, about her. How they met. How much they loved each other. None of it was true.'

She wasn't asking him to be wise. At least, he hoped not. He didn't have wisdom, he only had what was here, himself, her, the shelter of this place. He didn't want to abandon that. What could he say to her?

'I'm telling you what she said to me. Your father – maybe he told you what was true to him. Something else was true to her. You're here. I'm here. That's the truth. So – maybe that's what she meant.'

208

A slap of wind against them and her mouth clamped tight shut suddenly, she shook, she was trying to keep her teeth from chattering, although it was not so cold. Not like last night when they stood half-naked in the dark. The salt breath off the ripped surface of the sea, blown spray the fragments of secrets broken by travelling across oceans, through time, fractured by lies and collected up again in this place. The dwelling of stories, the dwelling of truth. He could have licked the spray off his collar, tasted the salt on his tongue.

'There was one story,' he said, 'about a woman who lived in a little cottage by the sea. She'd describe it, the fire grate, the small windows, a stone sink – it was so real to her. She looked at me, she held me –' Janet would have seen how he was lost in himself. He didn't care, he wished to give her this. What other gift could he give? 'It was the story of a woman whose husband had gone to sea, and her lover came back, and took her away on a great ship. She left her house, just like that. Left everything. Walked away and disappeared.'

He thought she would fall, just then, could almost hear the crack of her skull against the stones of the path, and so he moved to hold her. She let him, she was nearly falling, failing, but she would feel the warmth of him now, her thigh between his, her narrow shoulders in his grasp and his mouth close to the coil of her ear, the story-cup, listening, a strand of her sable hair against his lip. The scent rising from her, the track he'd left, an invisible scar.

'Left –' Her voice or his? Hers, brushed on the skin of his throat.

'Everything. Her whole life. More than her whole life.'

'The child.'

'A baby. A baby in a cradle, a baby asleep, a new baby, swaddled. And away she went.'

'Walked away.' Her tone was incredulous. He heard himself, when he was a boy. *She shouldn't have left that baby.*

'Out of the door, out of the house, down the path to the sea, to his ship. His ship was waiting in the harbour. It had sails of gold or sails of silver, I don't remember, but it was a ship from a dream, her lover's dream. She just stepped aboard. She left.'

'She left.'

Her echo of him. It was the sound of his own blood running, his own heart speaking. He held her close and closer. He could never protect her. How it fired in him then, the memory of what he'd wanted, wanted as a boy, as a child: to protect her, his mother. Her embrace had been marble, impenetrable, inviolable. He could not love her. She would not be loved. Her gaze was always far, far out to sea, to the horizon, looking for the end of one story and the beginning of another.

He wouldn't tell Janet that story's end, at least, not now. The cloven hoof, the cloven ship, the annihilating storm. He wouldn't tell her either how he'd waited here, wondering, opening and closing a door with a key he'd always had but never used, convinced as if by a vision that his mother would return, that they would meet here again at last, that she would not be able to keep away, that he would be the one standing on the threshold and she the one walking up the path. It had not turned out that way. Not quite that way.

Behind them, stretching inland, there was a wall of stones, laid lapped against each other, unsealed yet solid. Once the wall had been begun, by one pair of hands, or two, or five, and that might have been hundreds of years ago. But he himself had walked by more than once and kicked a fallen slab that had slipped loose from its anchor for reason or no reason. He would bend, lift the rough, lichened thing and see if he could find where it fitted, a crevice or hollow left incomplete. There. No. There. Yes. His own hands the same as those that had first made the wall, believed a boundary was necessary: Do not cross here. Wet moss leaving a stain on his skin. Just as easily he could have lifted stone after stone, unbuilding the work, breaking the bounds. No wall was too solid for that. It would take time, that's all. Holding Janet here, tight, the silver-sailed ship nearly visible on the sea, the boundary drew out at his back, ready to be breached.

* * *

Tom makes her finish the story that night. She knows he is cold, here outside by the rocks, hears his jaw snap open and shut, understands they must go back inside, and for the first time he is glad to be here, where there is at least some warmth from the fire she brings to life again. She takes his two hands in hers and rubs them between her palms, holding them in from the tiger-striped flame, crouching behind him, grinning, glad. But he does not stop shivering, she must hold him tight, so close against him that he can feel the shallowness of both their breaths, their ribs squeezed against each other, the hammering life in both of them.

It's too late, she says.

No, he says. *Please. This once.* She has put him in the bed, the ragged blankets, pink and black like dirty chewing gum, dragged up around his chin. Put him in the bed as if he were a baby in a cradle to be hushed and soothed and silenced. He won't be silenced, not tonight. He does not want silence. *Please*, he says again. *This once.*

I'm tired, she says.

He knows she has not slept. The image of her, not sleeping, arises at the back of his mind, the image of the stranger with his own pale hair. It was a dream, he tells himself quickly, a dream a dream a dream.

Then she gathers the rough corduroy of her warm skirt around her legs and climbs under the covers with him. There, she says. There. How's that?

He wants to swallow the story. She is so close: she could whisper into his mouth, not his ear. She draws her fingers through his dirty hair, over his temple and round the back of his neck. The bed creaks and their breath rises and falls in rhythm. He closes his eyes. He is not tired. He waits.

The spirit told her what he was, she says at last, not into his mouth but near enough, their cheeks close on the lumpy pillow. He can almost imagine they are somewhere else. It could be anywhere else. He wants to make the hewn walls, the flagstones, the queer blue people go. But the story is here. The story belongs here. There is no leaving. She is here.

He told her what he was, that he was not a spirit, but a man. Not a demon. A queen had got hold of him, a fairy queen, fallen in love with him, captured him – and now Tom could hear her smiling so he opened his eyes to see it. You remember, don't you, she said, not to believe what you read about fairies. Tiny spun-sugar girls in sparkly pink frocks and dragonfly wings. Not those kind of fairies, those are fake fairies. You remember, don't you?

Of course he remembers. He's known this a long time, as long as he's known anything, that the fairies were just the other folk, across the wall of the world, fierce and cruel and always jealous of human flesh. The fairy queen, the elf-queen; he'd met her before and before.

You could say it was strange that she loved him, she continues. Not the fairy queen. The girl, I mean. Loved the spirit who said he was a man, even though he'd whipped the rose from her fist so she'd been cut, dragged her will right out from under her, made her his by force, with the force of his spirit and flesh. But she loved him all the same. People will tell you, she says, and her voice is fierce, quick, hot, that nothing works this way. That it's only in stories. That it shouldn't happen. Don't believe it. It happens all the time. It happens everywhere you look.

If she has told him this story before, she has never told it in this way. This new telling forces the others away.

She could see he was a man, the girl could see it. Could see his fear and his weakness, how the wild queen would have carried him away as she had been carried away, and she felt soft for him in her heart as she felt soft for herself. That was what made the tears come, salt against both their skins because he held her close: his spirit-skin moved her heart and her body so that now her own will was returned to her and she kissed him.

A quick kiss on the boy's own mouth. Not a lover's kiss. But a kiss all the same. The heat of it runs through him and then evaporates or drifts away. The fire cracks, the wood resisting its fate.

The spirit who was not a spirit told the girl who was no longer a girl of the fairy queen's terrible love. For seven years she had kept him here her prisoner, to visit when she chose, to be the slave of her love, but now a new love had come and he would escape. The spirit flesh could fall from him, flayed off by human love. But it would not be easy, her spirit said. He had brought her inside his house, away from the spying wind which would carry their words back to the queen, the treacherous wind.

The tips of his fingers were cold when he brought them to

her cheek, but her tears warmed them. He licked the salt from his own skin, the human salt. You had courage to come here, he said. If you love me, you will need more courage still.

Love, the girl heard the spirit say. She did not know what it was. She felt torn and new-made, a spirit herself. Love, a word she had heard often and never thought of once. Courage, a word she had hardly heard. And yet she knew what that word meant.

* * *

It was only now that Tom understood the story his mother had told him. All the stories. The woman who had left for her lover's ship, the hunter and his seal-woman, that false knight, his father, whom they'd found here; and the story of the spirit who had been transformed by love. To abandon yourself was also a choice. It was not weakness. He saw himself burnt away with the lit blue gas, molten into metal, shaping what had been lost into something found but something kept hidden, too, faces of iron and steel, bodies of iron and steel locked away from sight, from daylight, even from his own unmasked gaze. Building himself a framework, a carapace. It seemed like nothing, now that he stood here on this shore with her. He had pushed at her, tormented her, shown her his possession, taken away hers. His own key, not hers. He had known, because of how he had lived, because of the child he had been, that there was something to wait for; she had known nothing. She was a gift, to him. What was he, to her?

'Why should I believe this either?' she said. She had pulled herself out of his arms and stood hugging herself instead. The skin under her eyes greenish with exhaustion.

'You could have made it all up. Found those pictures. I don't know. Stole this place, my house. Broken in. You're nothing to me. You could be nothing to me.'

'Is that what you want?' he asked. He knew it would be easier. It would not be terrible, if he were nothing, if he were not what he was, if they were not what they were, what they had become to each other. She didn't answer. Her eyes were too bright. He could see in her face then, the bald knowledge of what had passed between them, spilling out of her suddenly like a glass upended, a flood, a stain. Her legs went from under her, buckled. She sat down heavily, on the grass by the path, its coarse prickles, its yellow and green, marram and sea lyme, and when he knelt down by her he could smell the crushed verdure, the damp earth, the sickly catch of the gorse by the dunes in his throat. Far away from them the two seals split the sea, weaving in and out of each other's wakes, dancing and diving in the indigo waves, the black waves, the silver waves. The deck of the seal boat tilted, he hung on to the railing, the world tilted: he steadied himself in her seal-black eyes.

'Come on,' he said. 'Let's get back to the house. It's going to rain, anyway. Come on.' It was easy to be practical. He was good at being practical. There was always the next thing to do: it was as simple as that. He could imagine a whole life with her, built from one next thing after the other. He had seen her crush away her other life, wherever she had come from, knew that disappearance was wired into her as it had been wired into him. There was no escape from the desire to escape.

She stood. She was all right. Spits, drops, struck their cheeks; glistening on her lashes, her brow. No tears, only rain. 'Come on,' he said again.

They hadn't gone far from the house. How could they? It

215

held them both. He could not have known how much this path, this path back towards shelter that was no shelter, that was exposure, that was a void, he could not have known how much it reminded her of a path in a dream, a path through stilted ranks of yew, a path towards a grave. He could not have known: but he knew there was no grave, only the grave each of us makes for himself, the grave of belief, the end of the tale. His arm tight around her shoulder, he felt her shiver as if she rippled with the wind like the surface of the sea. Then she spoke. The steep slate roof of the house just ahead was darker now, slicked with wet, and the rain came harder. A cool lick of it ran down the back of his neck, and the path softened under their tread.

'My father just said that he loved her. That he loved her when he saw her. Right away, like that. Like you read about. He took her home with him. He used to tell me that story all the time, it was the one he liked best to tell. When he was happy. When it started. When everything was possible. Then he lost everything, I guess. Even I didn't make up for it, I don't think. I never asked him what had really happened to her, even though – I don't know any more, what I really felt. But I must have known there was something wrong. That if I asked too many questions, everything would break open, fall apart.'

The sudden flood of her words. He listened and held her.

'The stories we get told . . .' They were moving again through the rain. 'All we have to believe. So I came back here, to where she'd been. Of course I told myself I wasn't looking for anything, that it would be just a place, a thing I owned, four walls and a floor and a roof. I told myself it was chance, it was nothing. Everything is chance, nothing means anything. No choice you make has meaning. It's all random.'

'No,' he said to her. 'No.' He did not believe anything was random. If he had one belief, it was that. No chance. No accident. A journey towards a destination, even if the destination was behind a cloud, a dip in a hill, or down at the bottom of the sea. Now they had reached the green door. He stood and faced her. There was some shelter here, under what you could not call a porch but a lip of stone jutting out over their heads.

'Do you think it was only you she left?' he asked her. A ball of anger just above his breastbone. 'It wasn't only you. Maybe it's better not to know anything – did you ever think of it that way? Maybe it's better to have only what you imagine, what you think might have been. I remember when she left me.'

He could see just then how badly she wished to pull away, wished not to care or hear. Jerked like a kite in the wind of her desire, her desire to belong here but also to forget what she had done and what he had been, hours ago, a lifetime ago, their sweat, the taste of blood, the taste of a longing that could never be satisfied. The source of the desire was not present, but was in both of them; the source from which it had sprung. It was *her* they desired, she who had vanished from both of their lives, but they could only seek satisfaction in each other. It was good enough for him.

'Stop feeling sorry for yourself,' he said. He heard the harshness in his own words. 'Come inside out of the wet.'

* * *

Now, although the child Tom is curled in this hard bed, curled tight against her, when she speaks he sees so clearly the broad plain where they have been: the plain before the ruined castle where the fairies will ride.

The spirit had told her what she would have to do, the story went on. The story went on. There was always another story, another end, another beginning. He told her what she would have to do. She was to go at midnight, to the crossroads, and wait. Not alone: no, she and the baby he'd put in her belly, the two of them would go together. She was to wait in the moon dark, the dead cold, the wind that plucked at her clothes like a living thing. Wait until the bones of her feet were stones on the ground, the bones of her hands stiff twigs in her cloak, until her eyes were pearls from staring at nothing, at the empty plain, the crumbled ramparts. Wait.

If she waited, she would see them. And at last, yes, she did see them, streaming out from the broken mouth of that long-ago stronghold, and she was able to wonder, just for an instant, whether if she'd had the glamour of the fairy eye she'd be able to see it made whole again, the castle bold and solid. What she saw instead was a cavalry, the fairies' ride, great, green-eyed horses with flaming tails racing across the plain like stars falling from heaven, streaks of phosphored fear. She saw the queen at the head of that host, high on the black back of her mount and a sword upraised, her skull-grin, her red hair shot with sparks and her shadow on the moon which seemed to cower behind.

The girl had no breath, no heart. He had spoken a word to her, her lover, her spirit, this one who longed to be a man. What was that word?

There in the bed, the storyteller's arms tight around him like iron bands, the boy whispers the word to himself. He remembers the word. *Courage*.

Black horses, ink, coal, night, cavern black pouring by as if the night had been released out of itself: but then, through the charge, one white horse and her memory, too.

His spirit voice. *I was human, once,* he had said. *You will know me. Do not fear.*

One white horse with a bright body on its back, holding no sword but shrieking in a language that carved through her heart. Yet on her frozen feet she ran, ran to the white horse, sweat on her palms as she held her skirt high to free herself, to gallop as this army galloped, fearing nothing but herself. The moon horse, its rider, her grasp. Her white arm drawn like a blade from a sheath to cut him down, draw him down; he turned his head and she nearly let go when she saw the gaping fires of his imprisoned eyes turned on her in pleading. She dragged at him, dragged, and his skull cracked against hers as he fell from his horse to the ground, fell into her arms.

His voice: *Hold me tight and fear not.*

Heat roaring up at her, from the bar of iron he became, anvil-bright, nearly molten, ablaze. The howl of the raging queen, the howl of the furnace at her breast.

His voice: *Hold me tight and fear not.*

Cold now, worse than that, the shrinking, slithering, viridian coils of a serpent, fathoms long, fathoms long and drawn about her like a winding sheet so now she sent up a shriek of her own terror, she could not still herself, joining the cry of the wind, the clamour of the thundering, plunging, disordered army. The pits of the serpent's eyes, the swallowing dark.

His voice: *Hold me tight and fear not.*

Then the stink of meat-breath, a ragged mane, teeth ivory daggers at her neck, the devouring tongue and throat as red as the rose she'd pulled. His lion's claws threw clods from the earth and rent her cloak, her skirt, her shift, tearing and fighting her embrace, but she was red iron that had been forged, beaten, cooled. *Hold me tight and fear not,* fear not, until the beast's heat became another heat, her clothing torn so they were skin to skin, she and the spirit who had become a man again in her embrace, a naked man white on the plain, white in her arms, white in her love, her dear lover, her dear love.

Silent, it was suddenly silent on that wide, dark plain. The ruined castle still; the sea singing itself to sleep. Warmth in her arms, human warmth, and no sign but her torn clothing, but her human love, that any otherworld army had passed. No sign but one: for when she led him, slowly on his bare feet, they found a blade on the ground, broken in half and rusted through as if it had lain there since once upon a time, as if it had never been raised high in the fairy queen's grasp. Her lover stooped to pick up the pieces, and he threw them into the sea.

Then the silence of the storyteller's plain is the silence of this bed. The boy lies still. Opens his eyes. She presses his cheek against hers but he will not believe there are tears there. He kisses her neck. Happy ending, she says. Hold me tight, she says. Hold me tight and fear not. But the boy is already asleep.

* * *

Tom wished to offer proof of the possibility of transformation. That they could find what each knew, and did not know, in the other. When they got back into the house he set her again in the chair by the table; again he brought food, bread, cheese, just that, and the openmouthed knife with its carbon blade. Cut for her slices of each, but she did not move to touch them. Back in the scullery to make something hot for her to drink, coffee-grounds swirling away in cold running water, a quotidian sound. The rain ticked against the glass now. He went and put more wood on the fire.

'How old were you?' she said, finally.

He knew what she meant. When she left. 'I don't remember,' he said. 'Not exactly.'

Now tears filled her eyes and she looked tired, so tired.

'It wasn't a good time,' he said. 'It was a long time ago. *When* doesn't matter.' He knew, roughly. He had been thirteen, fourteen. How had he managed? He had found a way. He was clever, as she had been, at seeking out the cracks and crevices he could move into, at enlisting sympathy, at finding a place to sleep and something to put in his mouth. Waiting for discovery, finding what was necessary, escaping danger. Accepting danger, if it looked more appealing than safety. There were so many ways to see the world.

'And she just left.'

'Yes,' he said. 'She just left. What else could she do? She didn't stay long with you, I guess, because – I guess because she couldn't be away from here. You grew up –'

'On the other side of the world,' Janet said. 'My father took her away on a ship. That was the story. They crossed the ocean together. That's where I grew up.'

'Yes,' he said. It made sense to him now. She couldn't have gone far from here, or shouldn't have. Her spirit was here. He had seen it once in the shape of a man, his father; but it had not been separate from her, his mother, as Tom was not separate from Janet. There had been no choice. 'She made a mistake,' he said. 'Maybe she thought what I'd thought. What you'd thought. That she could get away. But she couldn't. I figured out – at least I think I did – that she would come and go, knowing she had to, maybe because of him. My father – and maybe for some other reason. She tried to stay away. I tried, too. I thought I'd find her again, here. I thought we would meet. She and I. But you and I did, instead. I knew she'd died, at least, I'm sure I did. Or knew you were coming. No difference. Not to me.'

'But what have we done?' The fear had come into her voice quick as a slap. Her eyes were the fairy queen's eyes, pits of rage, ashy with it, the heat of something that did not come from her, that seized her.

'What do you mean?' It was so simple to him. Really, it was. He had no doubt. But she was still leaving the world she'd known.

'I have a brother,' she said. 'I never knew I had a brother.'

It shocked him, almost made him laugh, how she simply turned her face from the table and was sick on the floor. The stuff spattered her boots, her jeans, the white gauze on her hand. She hadn't eaten much, nothing since last night, strings of kelpy bile flecked with bits of bread or cheese, he saw it pretty clearly. Her open mouth, her tongue, the mouth he wanted to kiss again. He wasn't disgusted. It made him love her more. This was what love was, at last and at last: of course. Love and fear, no difference between them, no distance.

Her hand on her belly. She knew what he had done, and so did he.

'Oh,' she said. 'Oh.'

Once more he saw it take her, the storm she made for herself, or that was made for her and of her. She sat up, fast, her head tipped back, and to steady herself, her right hand flat on the table. Her palm on the handle of the opened knife. Her eyes were shut; she was lucky, he thought, that her fingers did not catch the blade. Her open mouth and then her open eyes, full of her bright voltage. A trickle of saliva running from her lip to her chin, a silver thread like a spider's web. He reached out his hand to wipe it away – but he was not close enough. Left his chair. Knelt in front of her. Made his touch as light as he could, feathery, full of sweetness. He tried to call back the sweetness he'd felt as a boy, that rare magic, draw it into himself and then let it flow out again, flow towards her, the gift of his memory, of himself, of what they could be. What they could make.

He let his other hand rest on her belly. He kissed her, tasted the sourness, didn't care. Her eyes unclosing. Her back straight. How she had yielded to him. She was not yielding now. Where was she? He could not see into her gaze, her black gaze. He would always be looking for her, always wanting to crush her in his embrace to make her what he could love.

Hold me tight and fear not.

It happened very slowly, that he saw her take the knife in her hand. She'd woken from seizure, blinking back into this world, and curled her palm around its handle, the smooth yellow wood. Raised it, lifted it towards him, her eyes a metal mask, and it was strange how his heart rose too because in her desire for violence was the strength of her desire for him. But there was another way, another story. It had already begun and the ending, now, could not be changed. So he reached up to parry her, taking the blade of the knife in his own hand so his flesh opened, so he offered her his own weakness, his own blood, as her strength.

'Oh –' Her voice an open door. He saw her take in how she had injured him, a straight cut from the base of his middle finger to the rim of his wrist, saw her understand what she might have done (how easily anyone might say, *I'll kill him, I'll kill him*) and how she had drawn back from it, or been drawn back by him. There was no difference, because there was no difference between them. Does the tide draw at the sand or does the sand release the sea? He had felt her fear, mortal fear, of the love and blood they shared; it was fear that led her to rage and love that released her from fear.

And so she let go of the knife. It clattered to the floor, and he took her two hands in his (his mother, holding his hands, warming them, making him safe), a liquid warmth. He was smiling. He would love her, would keep her here, and she would allow herself to be kept, choose this. For a while or for ever, there was no time. She had put her arms around him now and held him, tight. This was how he would be loved, how he would be love itself. Opened by the metal edge of her, the stone of her. The sea of her. The distance travelled, the distance bridged. His blood ran into hers, of course it did. This was a story of blood, and blood would speak, would speak at last.

There is a lipstick on the dresser, by the cracked and clouded mirror. A tube of mock-tortoiseshell, twined with a relief of blossoms, a dull gold band where the lid can be drawn off with a sucking pop. In faded letters, just legible, on its base: Miss Firecracker. Two twists and then a finger of scarlet wax: red as blame. My breath blurs the air. It is cold here. The fire makes only a little warmth.

Whose face in the glass? It could be hers. I have tucked the photograph into the wooden frame: a black and white portrait, formal, a string of pearls, eyelashes retouched with a long fine brush. A closed-mouth smile, like mine. A dark clean gaze: you would call it candid, perhaps, unless you knew it was not. Our bones. Our eyes. Our throats.

I take the lipstick and press it to my mouth. Age has congealed it, made it sticky and chalky all at once, but I stretch my face and press, staining my lips with the colour. How easily we read wavelengths into monochrome: I know my lips match hers. I don't remember that mouth kissing me. I don't remember the smell of her perfume; I don't remember the click of those pearls near my ear as she kissed me goodnight. I have none of it. A sweet, chemical taste on the edge of my tongue.

I have something else, now.

My eyes half-shut, I tilt my head. Twins. The sky is

leached of colour so that out of the little window there is only black and white, the trees shadows against the shrouded sky. This could be a cut-out landscape, a set. The sea, with its secrets and seals, beyond. Here is my red mouth, here is blood unwashed from the blade of his knife, and his perfect stillness, his closed eyes. He is sleeping now. I will let him sleep. Soon I'll wake him, crawl in next to him and feel as if I am lying beside myself.

It seems to me that once I had another life; and soon, too, somehow, I will have to look for it. Not to recapture it. You can't recapture what was never real. When I came here I thought this was the dream, the other place I went to when I was seized, taken away from myself, made to vanish. But now I understand.

I am not the same as her, not quite the same. I will not disappear, not like that. But even if I did it wouldn't matter. Even if he came to find me – Stephen, that was his name – he would see that I was not what he thought he had known. There is nothing to be afraid of in that. Even he would see that nothing else exists but this.

Soon. Not now. Soon.